TO GLEN

book or chap scriptures say: 'Don't stop believin', hold on to that feeeliiin'—

Your bro from another mo,
David

Children of Eos

By David C. Silva

davidcsilva@shaw.ca

Copyright © 2016 David C. Silva

All rights reserved. This book or any portion thereof may not be reproduced in any manner whatsoever without the express written permission of the publisher except for the use of brief quotations in a book review.

This book is dedicated to my family; Grace, Philip, and Christina. Always remember that words create things. Keep speaking life into the world.

It is also dedicated to the memory of St. Maximilian Kolbe, Professor Mahmoud Al 'Asali of Mosul, Iraq, and Jamal Rahman of Ethiopia.

"We look forward to the time when the Power of Love will replace the Love of Power. Then will our world know the blessings of peace."

-William Gladstone

Table of Contents

Prologue		5
Chapter One	A Private Revelation	7
Chapter Two	The Triple Whammy	10
Chapter three	The Wizard of Eos?	20
Chapter Four	Meet and Greet	35
Chapter Five	The Nesting Stage	44
Chapter Six	First Day on the Job	55
Chapter Seven	A Voice in the Wilderness	59
Chapter Eight	A Priest and a Rabbi Walk into a Cave...	66
Chapter Nine	Return to Sender	70
Chapter Ten	Watch for the Curveball	79
Chapter Eleven	And the Oscar Goes to...	88
Chapter Twelve	Worst Case Scenario	96
Chapter Thirteen	Visiting Hours	104
Chapter Fourteen	Declaration of War	110
Chapter Fifteen	Redemption	119
Chapter Sixteen	Go Fish	125
Chapter Seventeen	The Veil is Lifted	129
Chapter eighteen	Requiem	134
Epilogue		138

Prologue

Awakened by the sound of a clanging pot and the savory smell of pan-fried potatoes, Jack fumbled for his pocket-watch. Groggily, he made his way outside the tent. In the dim light of morning, he could barely make out the time. A quarter past one, if his sleep-soaked eyes weren't deceiving him. He couldn't believe his brand-new timepiece wasn't working properly. He wished he could give Boston Watch Company a piece of his mind right now. The hands seemed to be moving fine, but the sun obviously doesn't lie.

He felt even more fatigued than usual this morning. Maybe gold mining wasn't his life calling after all. Maybe, he'd been deceived by the enchanting beauty of these majestic mountains. As he made his way to the campfire like an insect to the light, Alan, this week's designated cook, called out to him.

"Morning, lazy head, where's the rest of the crew?"

Jack took another look at his watch. It still seemed to be working fine. He held it up with his left hand, while pointing to the glare in the clouds with the other.

"Does the sun normally rise in the north at one o'clock in the morning?" Jack queried his workmate.

Alan took a few steps towards the watch, and poked his head forward to get a good look. He then turned toward the glare. Looking back at Jack, he was met with an equally puzzled and silent stare...

Meanwhile...over one thousand miles southeast of the Rockies, in Havana, Cuba, Antonio turned the key and locked up the tavern for the night. Normally, he would be going home much earlier, but there had been a big brawl just before closing time. It had taken him a lot longer than usual to clean up.

While walking along the narrow, cobblestone streets, a sudden whiff of Butterfly Jasmine grabbed his nostrils. He never tired of the familiar, soothing scent. It was the perfect antidote for the stale beer smell that seemed to linger in his senses. As he neared the intersection and a bigger part of the sky became visible, an eerie reddish glow caught his eye.

"My Lord...what is this?" he thought to himself.

His eyes told him it was beautiful, but in his heart, he felt it must be some type of omen; A good one, he hoped.

Later that day, in New England, a telegraph operator was taking a message from a grandmother in upstate New York. Suddenly, sparks began to fly, jolting her heart into race mode. What on Earth had come over the control board? She flipped switches futilely. She plugged and unplugged...but the system was dead.

What she, Antonio and the miners were all experiencing was 'The Carrington Event' of early September, 1856. A non-event really, unless you happened to be a telegraph operator or a sleep deprived early riser. Just the sun spitting up, as it regularly does, although this coronal mass ejection was larger than most. The huge solar storm it produced found Earth directly in its path. In the low-tech world of the nineteenth century, it went largely unnoticed.

What will be the outcome, not if, but *when* it happens again...?

Chapter One

A Private Revelation

Dan walked into the office and up to the receptionist.

"Hi, I'm here to make a payment and pick up an envelope." The young man with the jet-black hair grinned politely.

"And your name is?" the middle-aged woman asked.

"Daniel Goodrich."

"Ah yes, here it is."

She selected a white envelope from her desk drawer and handed it to him. Turning to her computer, she found the payment owing.

"Your balance is one hundred and fifty dollars."

He handed her the full amount in cash and waited for his receipt. "Thank you very much," she said with a smile.

"No...thank you." Dan assured her.

He took a quick, nervous look at the sealed envelope and walked out. It had cost him six hundred and fifty dollars in total to obtain this information, a lot of money for a barista. Even for one who worked in an upscale café frequented by big tippers.

Inside the elevator, he stared at the envelope all the way down to the lobby. When the door opened, the first thing to catch his eye was a large screen TV in the seating area. A much too uncaring looking anchorwoman, with much too perfect hair was commenting on the day's top story

"*Officials say the unprecedented swarm of twisters hitting the midwest shows no signs of abating. Indeed, forecasters say many more are expected to hit in the coming days.*"

Dan strolled up closer to the screen and watched intently, as the scenes of destruction flashed from one neighborhood to another.

"*With the National Guard and army reserves already stretched to the limit, government officials say regular troops may need to be called in soon to deal with the growing crisis.*"

As Dan turned away from the TV and headed for the doors, he murmured;

"Glad *I* don't live there."

When he arrived at his tiny bachelor pad, Dan plopped his backpack on the sofa and sat down beside it. There was no fireplace in his suite, and therefore no mantle on which to display his athletic awards. Instead, Dan used the top of his dresser to showcase his trophies. They were all for team achievements rather than individual awards. He was naturally athletic and could play almost any sport well. Maybe if he had focused on one particular discipline instead of being a jack-of-all-trades, he might have excelled at a certain sport. This pretty much summed up his whole life though. He had never felt like he really fit in anywhere, but he always managed to keep his head above water.

After unzipping the backpack, Dan pulled out the envelope and began another staring session with it. After a few seconds, he set it down on the coffee table in front of him and headed to the kitchenette. Inside the fridge, he found an ice-cold beer calling out to him. After grabbing it, he went back to the sofa, picked up the letter, and took a sip. It was like a bad car wreck. He simultaneously wanted to look, and at the same time keep going. He decided to keep going...for now. Back down went the letter on the coffee table, and on went the TV. It was set to the news channel, as it usually was at dinner time. Dan wasn't surprised to see coverage of the tornadoes dominating the headlines. However, something else quickly popped up to grab his attention, as he sipped on his beer

"*This is a breaking news story. NASA officials are informing us this evening that a massive solar-storm is headed directly toward Earth, and estimate that it should hit our atmosphere in approximately twenty-four hours.*"

The lady with the perfect hair now had Dan's full attention, as he wondered if this was a big deal or not

"We have Professor Joseph Mullins live with us now from NASA to give us the details...Professor Mullins, how exactly will this affect us?"

"Well Ann," the intelligent looking astronomer and spokesman replied. "There's good news and bad news. The bad news is, we're woefully unprepared for this even though we're overdue for it, and we've given warnings and recommendations to the government in the past. A solar-storm of this magnitude has the potential to cause massive damage to our infrastructures."

"...And the good news?" interjected the perky anchorwoman.

"The good news is that with the technology available to us today, we were able to see this baby coming from a mile away, or a little more precisely, about ninety-three million miles away. So, ahead of time, we can shut off the power grids, suspend air travel, etcetera," the seasoned astronomer replied.

"You're talking about temporary blackouts, am I right Professor?"

"Exactly Ann, but these are minor inconveniences compared to the alternative, which is trillions of dollars in damage," he warned.

"How long would these blackouts last exactly?" she pressed.

Shrugging, the mature looking official responded.

"There are various factors which we could only calculate during the event, but you'll be looking at a couple of days at least. But you also have to remember, that this will only mitigate the damage. All that energy has to go somewhere. Underground power-cables will be especially vulnerable..."

Dan wondered how minor an inconvenience this would be for him, as he enjoyed his ice-cold beer. It had been a hot, late summer afternoon. Dan knew beer was not the best form of hydration, but it sure felt good going down. He was quite thirsty, and the feel of the bittersweet fizz in his throat felt very satisfying.

Dan had lived in Albuquerque all of his twenty-two years, and the one time he had travelled out of state was when his foster parents took him to Disneyland at the age of fourteen. He was completely accustomed to the high altitude. However, he had only been drinking for a few months. Whether it was the novelty of having alcohol in his system, or the altitude intensifying the effects, Dan wasn't sure. All he knew was that drinking made him drowsy, very quickly. A fact that had not gone unnoticed by his friends, who teased him about it mercilessly.

He put down the nearly empty can and put his feet up on the coffee-table. The last thing he remembered seeing was an advertisement touting the benefits of reverse mortgages. And with that, he was off to dreamland.

Chapter Two

The Triple Whammy

"There you go, skinny latte, extra shot." Dan smiled, as he passed the steaming cup to his last customer.

"Thanks," replied the yuppie in the grey business suit.

As he walked out of the café, Dan followed him to the door, locked it, and flipped over the open sign. Normally, the café would close at nine, and it was only three in the afternoon, but it was now Thursday and the scheduled blackout was coming at three-thirty. As he was quickly cleaning the tables, Dan heard his manager call out from behind the counter.

"That's okay, I finish cleaning up, you go home now!" said the olive skinned, balding Italian.

"Thanks Mister Zanetti," Dan said as he removed his apron.

Since transit service was temporarily suspended as well, Dan had to walk home. He was saving every penny he could for college, and having a car would put a serious delay in those plans. Fortunately, he only lived twelve blocks away. And they were rather short city blocks, not like the long stretches in the suburbs.

Dan was halfway home when he noticed all the lights go off at exactly three-thirty. It didn't make much difference to him since it was still broad daylight. He did however have to be careful crossing the streets, since he wouldn't have the aid of traffic lights.

About four blocks from home, he was thinking about all the preparations he had made the night before; candles, matches, baked goods when he suddenly heard what sounded like a scream coming from inside a nearby store. It seemed to have come from Donegan Jewellers, just up ahead. As he approached the store, Dan could see the sign said closed, but that there were still people inside. He tried the door despite the sign, and it pushed open. As soon as he entered, he was yelled at.

"Can't you read?" yelled a scruffy looking man with a ski-mask.

Dan found himself staring right down the barrel of a handgun. However, even in the dim daylight he could see a small red spot on the rim. He wasn't normally this observant, but his eyes were frozen in the right place just by chance. Was it a real gun? It seemed more plastic than metallic. Or was it just the lack of good lighting that made it appear so?

"Well...are you gonna wait till I shoot, or are you gonna leave?" the increasingly agitated fellow said with a growl.

This broke Dan's trance. He took his eyes away from the gun, and toward the young lady behind the counter. All he could see was that she had dark hair, and looked terrified. The robber held her by her longish hair with his left hand, like a dog on a leash, ready to yank on it if she disobeyed.

As with many people, when faced with a sudden and dangerous dilemma, Dan simply didn't have time to react. By now, the adrenalin was in full flow. He leapt from a standstill, directly at the arm of the intruder, and grabbed his forearm with both hands. Dan's average build belied his actual strength. His athleticism had come in very handy indeed. In his mind, Dan could almost hear a gunshot. But in reality, there was none.

The gun dropped to the ground and bounced about with very high-toned taps. As soon as the thief released his fistful of hair and punched Dan, the clerk reached for the small fire extinguisher which hung directly behind her. Dan took the punch to the forehead in stride, then threw one of his own. It landed directly on his foe's right cheek and sent him reeling backwards against the counter. Wasting no time, Dan pounced on him and grabbed him by the collar with both hands, ready to throw him to the floor while he was still off balance.

Unfortunately, albeit with helpful intent, the young lady decided to take a wild swing at the assailant with her newfound weapon. Her goal was to smack him on the side of the head, hopefully ending the whole ordeal. The actual landing point of the canister was somewhere between Dan's left hand and the man's neck. Dan immediately released him and grabbed his throbbing hand with his good hand. The young jeweller quickly lifted the extinguisher for a second strike, but the would-be robber realized he had just been gifted an opportunity. He decided to abort his failed attempt at instant wealth. With Dan temporarily out of commission, the thug ran out of the store fast enough to make a jackrabbit jealous.

"Are you okay?" the relieved clerk asked.

Dan quickly shook his sore hand in the air a few times.

"Yeah. How about you?"

"Just missing a few hairs, otherwise, I'm fine," she said.

Dan grabbed his cellphone and dialled for help. A message quickly came up stating that it was searching for service.

"Not now!" he complained.

"Are you forgetting about the blackout?" she reminded him. "The service providers will all be down for a while."

"Then why is my phone still on?" Dan wondered.

"Because you haven't turned it off?" the smiling young woman timidly pointed out, seemingly afraid of offending his intelligence.

Dan smiled and shook his head before confessing.

"What was I thinking?"

"You probably weren't, with all that just happened," she said sympathetically.

"Are we supposed to turn them off, so they don't blow up or something?" Dan asked.

"No, they're too small and weak to be affected by the electromagnetic waves," she informed him.

"So, you're smart as well as pretty," Dan suggested.

With the expression of a flattered schoolgirl, she smiled and extended her right hand.

"My name is Evelyn, but you can call me Eve."

Shaking her soft hand, he countered somewhat shyly, "My name is Daniel, but you can call me Adam."

Eve giggled and groaned simultaneously, like one does when hearing a bad joke.

"Not funny, huh?" Dan grinned.

"Well, it was funny the first time I heard it," she consoled him. "At least you have a sense of humor. That's one of the assets."

"You mean there's an official list?"

"I mean...that's...*an* asset," she corrected herself nervously.

"Thanks," Dan said. Obviously, the landlines are down as well, so I guess that guy's gonna get away clean," He lamented, as he bent down to pick up the gun.

It was light and made of plastic. The robber had obviously painted over the red rim, but had either missed a spot, or it had been chipped away.

"Just as I thought...and hoped," he said. "It's a toy."

"How could you tell?" Eve wondered.

"I wasn't sure, but this red spot here made me wonder," Dan replied.

"Well, it's the thought that counts. You risked your life to help me," Eve assured him. I was absolutely petrified, I had no idea what his intentions might be. As far as I'm concerned, you tried to save my life."

Dan just looked into her brown eyes, which matched her hair color as he could now see, until it turned into an awkward stare.

"Here, let me help you clean up," he offered as he bent down again. This time, he picked up a ring and handed it to her on bended knee.

"Are you proposing to me?" Eve grinned slyly, exposing the subtle dimples in her cheeks.

"Huh?" was the only thing Dan could say as he instantly realized what he'd just done, and felt a bit stupid for setting himself up.

"Relax, I'm just kidding. I also have a sense of humor...Adam."

The two then shared a long laugh, as they picked up other pieces of jewellery dropped in the confusion. Once everything was back where it should be, the two looked at each other and shared another awkward stare, until Eve broke the silence.

"Thanks again Daniel, I owe you big time."

"It's Dan...you can call me Dan," he corrected her. "And you don't owe me anything. I'm sure anyone would have done the same thing."

Eve disagreed. "I wish you were right Dan, but I think people like you are in short supply nowadays."

She then reached behind the counter and grabbed a business card and a pen. She quickly jotted down her full name Evelyn Donegan, and her phone number.

"If you like, you can call me some time, when the phones are working again," she said as casually as she could act, trying to not let her eagerness show.

Dan accepted the card and looked at it.

"I will," he said, before slipping it into his pants pocket. "Well, you better get home before it gets dark," he advised her. "I only live a few blocks away from here myself."

"Are you walking?" she asked.

"Yeah, I'll be home in like, five minutes."

"The least I can do is give you a lift," Eve offered opportunistically.

"Sure," Dan gladly accepted as he held the door open for her.

Inside Eve's BMW, Dan felt a little out of place, and he quickly hid his inadequacy with small talk.

"I can't believe that guy didn't even wait for nightfall."

"Well, we don't know exactly when the power will suddenly come back on, along with the alarms and surveillance cameras," Eve suggested.

"That makes sense," Dan realized. "...And here we are. He pointed to the light beige apartment building, as the car came to a stop. "I live in 301, that's my window right there.

"So, you live alone...?" Eve wondered.

"Yeah, my parents don't live around here anymore."

"That wasn't what I meant," Eve clarified abashedly.

"Oh yeah, sorry...I live alone. If you're ever in the neighborhood, just give me a buzz."

"I'll do that," she replied with a sincere nod.

"Thanks for the lift," Dan said as he stepped out of the car. "I'll call you sometime."

"Please do," Eve said with a big smile.

After exchanging waves and watching her drive off, Dan headed for the front door. He had wanted to invite her in, but he didn't have the courage. Besides, the darkness would only have added to the awkwardness of the situation.

Once inside, Dan lit some candles that were already prepared for this moment. On the table was a bag of cheese-buns, and the still sealed envelope he'd picked up two days before. He opened the bag and removed a bun. Taking a quick glance at the unopened letter, he sank his teeth into the somewhat still fresh bread.

On the other side of town, Eve was arriving home. She also lived in an apartment, but it was a much more luxurious dwelling than Dan's. It was a fifteen hundred square foot suite with a solarium, full sized kitchen, Jacuzzi, and a Mediterranean themed décor. At barely twenty-one years of age, she seemed to be doing very well for herself. Her parents had owned a chain of jewellery stores, and since Eve was an only child, she had inherited everything. Of course, she would gladly give it all up, if doing so could bring them back. After walking from the front door to the living-room, lighting candles along the way, she reclined on the large, cream colored sofa and slipped off her shoes. Putting her feet up onto a big fluffy cushion, she let out a deep sigh.

"Well, that was an exciting day!" she exclaimed aloud, before turning her head toward the salt water aquarium. Inside the oversized tank, yellow Angelfish and Powder Blue Tangs glided amongst the Sea Fans and multi-colored Coral. Eve threw her long, brown hair back, and gazed intently into their peaceful, watery world.

***

In his sixty-seven years of existence, the Chief had seen many wondrous, natural sights; terrifying thunderstorms, spectacular meteor showers, gorgeous sunsets, even a tornado. One of the things he had never witnessed before, were the Northern Lights.

As he gazed up from his perch, atop the sandstone cliffs, he was in complete awe. Against the perfect backdrop of a clear night, luminous sheets of green and purple hues intermingled gracefully. He enjoyed good fireworks displays as much as the next person, but this was different. There were no loud cracks of exploding gunpowder, no smoke. There was only the pure and silent dancing, of heavenly streams of light.

He raised his arms and offered up a sacred chant. It was a prayer of thanksgiving, and for beseeching future divine providence. Coincidentally, or not, wolves began to howl in unison with the aboriginal man's lead vocals. It seemed that nature had provided him with back-up singers.

***

In the morning, the bright sunshine gave the city a false appearance of normalcy, as an older looking blue sedan pulled up in front of Eve's apartment. When she stepped out the front entrance and saw the car, she noticed a sixtyish looking African-American dressed like a door to door salesman from the fifties step out. His suit matched the car perfectly. Was that who she thought it was? Indeed, when he noticed Eve and called out to her, she knew for certain it was him.

"Eve...good morning!"

"Michael!"

"I'm so glad I caught you before you left for the shop. It saves me a trip," he said happily, as Eve greeted him with a smile.

"Long time no see!"

But what on Earth was he doing back now, and so early in the morning? They kept walking toward each other and shared a quick, polite embrace.

"It's great to see you again, what brings you around these parts?" Eve wondered.

"I'm afraid it's time to gather," Michael stated quite bluntly.

"Gather?" she asked, exchanging the smile on her face for a look of bewilderment. "Is it because of the blackouts?" she guessed. "They said they can probably turn the power back on sometime tonight."

"I'm afraid that won't be happening Evelyn."

He always called her by her full name whenever he wanted her full attention.

"Why not?"

"Because they already did, a few hours ago. Some areas had power restored for a couple of minutes. Most people were still asleep and didn't even notice."

"A couple of minutes?" Eve echoed confusedly. "Then what happened?"

"Well," he said. "Our inside intelligence tells us that some hostile foreign entity exploded a nuke high over our atmosphere, causing a powerful EMP that knocked out most of the power grids. Unlike the sunburst which gave us plenty of heads up, by the time we knew what was happening, it was too late. It's a big mess Evelyn," he added bluntly.

"So how long will it be before they can fix it?" she asked naively.

Michael realized she wasn't grasping the full extent of the situation, and educated her further.

"Evelyn...most of the country is shut down. It will take billions of dollars and many months or even years before everything is back to the way it was. It doesn't help that the authorities were already at full stretch with the weather disasters, damage from the solar hit, and all the looting. Whoever did this, kicked us when we were down. Strategically, it was brilliant timing. They did maximum damage."

Eve now understood, and had a sudden, shocking thought.

"Does this mean that we're militarily vulnerable right now?"

"Oh... no," he reassured her, raising and lowering his hands as if to say calm down. "The government takes care of its own. They have preventative measures and backups to deal with such things. Unfortunately, we can't say the same about all the power companies, financial centers, fuel companies, telecommunications, etc. No Evelyn, at this point we're still a nuclear superpower. Ironically, it's our own fellow citizens who will quickly become our worst enemies."

By now, in a state of near shock, she meekly accepted his prognosis. "Okay, so what's my next step?" she asked.

Michael clasped both her shoulders with his hands.

"I'm assuming you have the manual handy?"

Eve quietly nodded in the affirmative.

"Okay, just follow it step by step, and don't dilly-dally. Give yourself enough time to get to Eos before sunset. I give it about a day and a half max, before everyone realizes the situation and starts fighting over food and water. I'll see you there. I have three more on my list that I have to find. Good luck," he said, squeezing her shoulders before heading toward his car briskly.

After watching him leave, Eve turned and headed right back into the building, in a much more hurried pace than she had earlier exited.

***

Dan awoke feeling unusually refreshed and alert, considering he wasn't a morning person. Without any electronic distractions, he had gone to sleep much earlier than usual, and got an extra couple of hours sleep in the process. He immediately wondered if the power was back on. He sat up in his sofa-bed and reached for the remote control. After pressing the power button a few times fruitlessly, he concluded the batteries might be low again. He stood up and headed for the light switch. There was the usual flicking sound, but no light. He walked over to the fuse box on the wall and pried it open. All the switches seemed to be in the on position. He toggled the switch marked living-room off, and back on again, then made his way back to the light switch. Still nothing.

"Aww...man..." he whined. "How am I supposed to make coffee?"

After taking a quick, cold shower, Dan put on his white dress-shirt and black pants. He had decided to just head to work a little earlier. Once there, he could maybe eat something. Hopefully the power would be back on by then, or shortly thereafter. Besides, the quality of the coffee would be better than anything he was used to at home. He combed his short hair with the aid of a handheld mirror in front of the living-room window, the only place that was bright enough. Suddenly, he heard a tap on the pane. Dan looked down to the street and was surprised, but in a pleasant way, to see Eve waving at him. Since the buzzer wasn't working, she had thrown a pebble at his window. He smiled and waved back. She then motioned for him to come down, which he promptly did. Stepping outside, Dan squinted as his eyes adjusted to the bright morning sunlight.

"Hi, what a pleasant surprise!" he beamed, as Eve met him at the entrance.

"Good morning," she replied with a very nervous look.

"Is everything okay?" Dan asked sincerely.

"Kind of," she answered coyly. "Can I come upstairs?"

"Of course," he said, as he opened the door for her.

Led by Dan, the pair made their way up the dark stairway quickly but quietly. At one point, Dan turned back to look at her, hoping she would say something. But she didn't. It seemed like whatever she had to say was for his ears only.

It was only once they reached his suite...at that very moment, that Dan realized he was a bit of a slob.

"I'm Sorry about the mess," he said apologetically, as he shut the door. "You caught me off guard."

Eve did a quick scan of the apartment, then turned to him.

"Oh, don't worry about it, it's not that bad."

"So, what brings you to my humble abode, my lady?" Dan said in a playful manner, hoping to ease what he felt was some tension in the air.

Eve didn't seem amused in the slightest. She just stared at him for what seemed to Dan like a minute, but was actually a couple of seconds. Dan was just admiring how nice her slim figure looked in her form-fitting, bright green dress, when she blindsided him with a most unusual question.

"Um...I know this is going to sound really, really weird but, how fast can you pack up your prized possessions into a small suitcase?"

Dan was mystified and quite shocked.

"Why?" he asked, smiling in a way that made him look afraid to hear the answer.

"I want you to come away with me for a while," was her startling reply.

Dan suddenly felt a wide range of emotions all in the same moment; amazement, flattery, confusion...and concern. Was she suffering from some sort of post-traumatic symptoms?

"Is this about what happened yesterday at the jewellery store? Do you need to talk about it?" Dan asked in a sympathetic manner.

Eve quickly caught on to where he was headed.

"What? No...I haven't gone nuts. At least not in the clinical sense." She couldn't believe she still had a sense of humor even at a time like this, she thought to herself. "This has nothing to do with the robbery," she asserted adamantly. "It's a long story. If you'll just trust me and start packing, I'll explain. It's all for your own good. Can you please just trust me?" she pleaded.

Dan sensed she was on the verge of crying. He would do almost anything to avoid such an emotional situation, so he decided to humor her. Besides, for some inexplicable reason, he *did* trust her. Dan didn't understand how he could trust someone he had just met yesterday, but he did.

He went to his one and only closet and pulled out a faded blue suitcase. He then set it down on the sofa and opened it. It looked as if it had been abused by former discus throwers, turned baggage handlers. However, it was sturdy and light, and Dan was a rather practical person. Besides, when you're on a tight budget, esthetics are not always a consideration. As he went back to the closet and began digging around, Eve positioned herself about halfway between the closet and the sofa. She then started to elaborate.

"Okay, here's the situation. Somebody, somewhere, acquired or got control of a nuke and exploded it over the U.S. early this morning." Dan stopped what he was doing and looked at her. "Most of our infrastructures are fried," she continued. "This blackout will last for a very long time."

"Eve, this blackout was caused by the solar storm...remember?"

"No!" she quickly shot back. "They turned the power back on a few hours ago, or at least some of it. A few minutes later the EMP from the missile blast disabled most of the country's electronics!"

The look on Dan's face made her feel like a babbling idiot.

"Why did you stop packing?" Eve asked with a serious tone.

Dan pulled some dusty papers from the closet shelf and headed to the sofa. Continuing to play along, he placed them in the bottom of the suitcase before walking to the dresser.

"Couldn't they see a missile coming from halfway across the world and prepare for it?" he asked.

"Well I'm no expert on these things, but I know they can fit missile launchers onto shipping containers. It could have been fired right off the coast for all we know."

"So, we're running from the fallout?" he asked, opening the drawer.

Eve didn't skip a beat.

"No, it was one blast, and high in the atmosphere. The air currents will disperse the radiation and carry it God knows where. That's the least of our worries right now."

Dan kept packing and at the same time trying to figure out exactly what it was that they were running from.

"So why are we leaving then?"

"Well we could just stay here and wait for your neighbors to come and steal your mac and cheese..."

Eve immediately realized that Dan might take her statement as a jab against his financial conditions. She hoped that's not how he took it. For his part, Dan was sure of only one thing, she honestly believed what she was telling him. For some reason, that was enough for him to keep packing.

"And where exactly are we supposed to go?"

"Eos!" was her quick and simple reply.

"Isn't that in Greece?"

"What?" I don't know. You're probably thinking of Greek mythology, that's where the name comes from. Eos was the god of the dawn. It's the name for a secret place about four or five hours from here."

Dan almost stopped packing again, but didn't want to create any more tension. Evidently, she was living out some kind of secret-agent fantasy or something. After snapping the latches of the suitcase into place, he reached for the remote. He pointed it determinedly at the small TV, hoping it would come alive. The lady with the soft, manageable hair would appear, she would explain how everything was back to normal, and Eve would snap back into reality. Instead, the futility of his attempt was met with disbelief by his agitated houseguest.

"What are you doing?" she snapped immediately. "We have a long drive ahead of us, let's go!"

Dan threw the remote onto the sofa, grabbed his suitcase, and headed for the door. He then stopped in his tracks and turned around. He grabbed the envelope that was still on the kitchen table, folded it once, and stuffed it into his jacket pocket. Somehow, Eve had made him forget about it for the first time since it had come into his possession. She quietly watched as she waited in the doorway, with a *'will you puh...leeze hurry up'* look on her face.

Chapter three

The Wizard of Eos?

After placing Dan's suitcase in the trunk of Eve's car, the two drove off, heading east. A trailing cloud of dust quickly formed behind them.

"You know, I'm supposed to be at work in about forty-five minutes," Dan informed his driver.

"Where do you work by the way?" she asked curiously, ignoring his concern.

"Over at Zanetti's café. That's where I was coming from yesterday, when I came into your shop."

"Oh, that's cool," Eve said sincerely. "But unless they have a diesel generator, they'll be closed for business for a long time."

Dan secretly hoped this adventure would be over by the end of the day, regardless of any work obligations and such, as he continued to question Eve.

"So, this Eos place is about three hundred miles from here you said?"

"Roughly," she replied.

"And I'm assuming the gas stations are all closed?" he reasoned.

"Correct," she answered, knowing what he was thinking. "Don't worry, I know where to go for fuel. We're headed there now."

Of course, Dan thought to himself. *What secret agent worth their salt wouldn't be ready for an emergency?* He looked down at the fuel gauge. There was about half a tank left. Things were going to get very interesting quite soon enough he assumed, as Eve pointed down in front of her passenger.

"Can you please hand me the black manual from inside the glovebox."

As Dan opened it, she pulled into the driveway of a rather shabby looking rancher. They were now in the outskirts of town. She received the booklet from his hands and stepped out. Dan followed behind curiously. She looked over to him nervously, like she was about to speak, then turned again and headed for the front door. She knocked quickly and assertively, then looked inside the manual. A few moments later, a strong, male voice called out from inside.

"Who is it?"

Instead of responding, Eve knocked five times, then paused about one second. She then knocked once and paused again momentarily before knocking five more times. As she was closing the book, the door opened.

"Eve, is it? I've been expecting you," said the hillbilly as he opened the door.

At least that's how he appeared to an absolutely dumbfounded Dan, who looked like a fish on a hook once the angler has it in hand. The large man immediately looked over to Dan, then at Eve.

"Who is this?" he asked with a surprised and concerned look.

Eve smiled anxiously. "Oh... this is Daniel. He's the latest, and obviously the last, of the chosen ones from our area. His mentor just approved him yesterday."

The bearded giant in overalls smiled and extended his hand toward him. Dan was by no means short at six feet, but he felt small in front of this behemoth. Being a few inches shorter than Dan, Eve must have felt like a child.

"Welcome aboard young man, my name's Jimmy. Don't worry, everything's gonna be fine," he said, noting the scared look on Dan's face as he accepted the firm handshake.

"You two are a little overdressed for the occasion, don't you think?"

"Oh, we were both on our way to work," Dan pointed out.

"Follow me," Jimmy said with a sudden spring in his step.

After leading the couple to the side of the house, Jimmy unlocked a large shed and quickly entered. He soon came out with two large jerry-cans of gasoline. He handed them one each and told them to return for more.

As Dan followed Eve back to the car, a very scary thought suddenly entered his confused mind. Was it possible that this was all for real? What was all this talk about chosen ones and mentors? Had he somehow managed to get himself involved with some doomsday cult or something? Dan hoped that they were no more than some overeager survivalists. Were they headed for some sort of camp? Dan's brain went into overdrive as a multitude of questions now flooded his mind. He couldn't help wondering about what kind of people awaited them at this Eos. He thought about the terrorist attack Eve had alluded to, and wondered if the situation was as bad as she had made it out to be. While his mind raced, his mouth remained tightly sealed, as he followed Eve back and forth between the car and the house.

After moving the suitcases into the backseat to make room for the last gas can, they were quickly sent on their way by their fuel supplier.

"Go on, give yourself enough time for a bathroom break or two!" Jimmy said loudly, as he tapped the side of the car twice with his open palm.

Dan was glad they didn't have time to chat. He wouldn't have known what to say, if he was asked about his mentor and such.

Within minutes, they were on the main highway heading out of town toward the south. By now, the Albuquerque skyline had been reduced to gleaming specks in the distance, but the mountains remained prominent on their left side. Eve noticed how they always seemed to have a different color, depending on the time of day and the season. Right now, they were dressed in an earthy ochre hue that contrasted beautifully with the clear azure skies.

Dan figured the straight drive, without traffic lights and stops, would be a good time to get some details. Without turning his head toward Eve, he began to grill her.

"So, I'm a chosen one?"

"Well, kind of. ...I chose you."

"Does that mean you're my mentor?" Dan asked her.

Eve appeared somewhat hesitant in her response.

"Well I'm mentoring you, so I guess I am. Although, I'm not officially a mentor."

"And just who would that be, officially?" he wondered.

Eve explained the process to him.

"There are many mentors throughout the country. Each one is responsible for a geographic area, which is based on population size. My mentor's name is Michael. He's the one who came to me this morning, to let me know the gathering had begun."

"And how do you apply to become a chosen one?" Dan couldn't help but ask.

"Oh, you don't find them. They find you," she educated him. "They basically go around scouting people for potential candidates. If they think you may be suitable then they do a series of tests on you, without you even knowing it. If you pass these tests, then they approach you and explain who they are."

"How can they test someone without them even knowing it?" Dan wondered.

Eve now began to speak in a more relaxed manner, as she sensed that Dan was finally coming to accept the whole affair.

"It's pretty simple really. For example, one time I found this wallet with a pretty big wad of cash in it. Just cash and a card with a name and address. So, I took the wallet to the address, and who do you think came to the door?"

"Michael?" Dan guessed.

"That's right. He then introduced himself and explained how I had been selected for a special study, without giving much detail. Once he was sure I was suitable, he elaborated on the whole Eos project. After I let him know I'd be willing to be a part of it, he gave me this manual. He basically instructed me to just go about life as usual, and if the day ever came to gather at Eos, I would be contacted then."

Dan still couldn't see how she would agree to be involved with something so radical.

"So, you agreed to leave your family and friends behind, should the need arise?"

"I'm actually an orphan. My parents died in a car accident a few years ago," Eve disclosed.

Dan felt bad about his accusatory tone, and he could sense that she was still not over the loss, not surprisingly.

"I'm so sorry to hear that. I wish I could take back what I just said."

"Don't worry about it, you didn't know. As for leaving people behind, you have to realize that going to Eos is kind of like going to college. It's a place to acquire skills and knowledge. The whole purpose is to train us to become self-sufficient leaders. When we're ready, we can go back into the outside world and help rebuild it. We're of little use to our loved ones if we don't know how to help them. Also, they purposely select people who they feel don't have family responsibilities. Besides, they're not responsible for any breakdowns in society. Eos is a solution, not a problem."

"How do you know I don't have any sick friend or relative who needs me, or a girlfriend I didn't want to abandon?"

"Because you would have told me so back at the apartment, and you wouldn't be here right now."

Dan knew she had a great point, and he had no argument for her. He realized that she had thought long and hard about the situation, but he still yearned for more details.

"Exactly who came up with the idea for such a place, and what does it look like?" he asked.

Eve shrugged a little before answering.

"All I can tell you is that it was created by the chief caretaker, whom I've never met. And I haven't seen the exact location either. The complex consists of some hidden caves that were used a long time ago by the Native Americans."

Dan was by no means claustrophobic, but the idea of living in a cave didn't seem very appealing.

"Most of it lies inside the Gila National Forest," she continued. "In and around the caves there are many sources of clean water, edible plants, fish and some wild game. Also, the entrance is on a large private estate, where many crops are grown. In the manual, it says there are these people called caretakers. They actually live there and maintain the whole place. There are also guardians, who are basically security guards."

Eve picked up the manual from beneath the car radio, and handed it to Dan.

"Here, read all about it. There are some maps in the back of it too."

Before opening it, he just had to ask one final, nagging question.

"Since I'm not officially a 'chosen one,'" he said, making air-quotes with his fingers, "how will we be received when we get there?"

Without saying a word, she took a quick look at Dan, then stared ahead quietly. Her silence in no way inspired confidence in her passenger.

After pondering the whole situation quietly for a few awkward moments, Dan suddenly verbalized his thoughts.

"Why did you decide to bring me along anyway?"

Breaking her silence, Eve answered immediately.

"Because you saved my life."

"That gun was fake, remember?"

"Like I said before," Eve insisted, "It's the thought that counts. And compassion for your fellow man and bravery are both assets."

Dan remembered her same comment earlier, about his sense of humor.

"So there really is an official list?"

"Yeah..." she confessed.

"Okay, so how do you know I possess all these qualities?" Dan challenged her.

Eve took another one of those looks at him, before refocusing on the road ahead. This time however, she answered promptly, albeit somewhat meekly.

"I just know it," was her simple answer.

Although Dan felt sincerely honored and flattered by her assessment, he just couldn't let it go at that.

"I really appreciate what you're trying to do…but I don't want to get you into any trouble. You need to just drop me off somewhere, and go on by yourself."

Eve's eyes opened wide.

"Are you nuts?' she exclaimed. We're in the middle of nowhere! I am *not* leaving you by yourself!"

"I can take care of myself. I'll just hitch a ride back home, or wherever seems safe right now," Dan insisted.

Just as Eve opened her mouth to respond, a siren suddenly began blaring behind them.

"What did I do?" Eve asked, looking down at her speedometer.

"They're probably just checking on us, to make sure we're safe and all." Dan assumed. "There aren't as many cars on the road as usual, he added.

As Eve pulled over, he flipped to the maps in the back of the manual. Eve looked in her rear-view mirror, as two men exited the police car behind them.

"Here we go!" Dan exclaimed. "There's a small town really close by. I'll ask the police about it. Maybe I can even bum a ride."

As the two men approached, one on each side, Eve took a look in her side-mirror. She suddenly put the pedal to the metal, and took off in a screaming cloud of dust and burnt rubber.

Dan dropped the manual, and his jaw, as he jerked his head toward Eve. He then took a quick look behind, to see the two men running back to their car. Looking back to Eve with disbelief, he yelled at her.

"What the hell are you doing?!"

"Those aren't cops!" she screamed nervously, with the same scared look she'd had during the robbery.

"What do you mean they're not cops?" Dan demanded to know.

With her eyes shifting between the road and the rear-view mirror, she explained herself.

"They're not in uniform, and they look scruffy and mean."

"How do you know they weren't undercover?"

"Why would they use a marked patrol car if they were undercover?" she reasoned. "And, don't they have their hands full with the outages and everything? Besides, I wasn't even speeding or swerving, or anything. If they stole our gas, we'd be stuck in no man's land between home and Eos. Not to mention what might happen if they got their hands on that manual!"

Dan took a quick peek behind. They were in hot pursuit. He then looked over at the fuel gauge.

"Well, whoever they are, I hope they have less than a quarter tank, or we're sitting ducks."

Dan fully expected to hear gunshots from behind, or for a helicopter to suddenly swoop down on them. His fears were not to be realized however, as no further drama came to pass. For the next five minutes, they drove quickly toward their intended destination, without exchanging a word. The cruiser followed closely behind them. Whether that car was staffed with real police officers or not, would never be known for certain. The next time Eve looked in the rear-view mirror, she noticed the pursuing vehicle was getting smaller and smaller. It soon faded away and melted into the landscape. She decreased her speed, just a little, and released a sigh of relief.

"Thank God! They gave up!" she exclaimed.

To make sure, Dan turned himself around and checked with his own two eyes.

"Great. We should pull over soon and refuel." Dan stated as calmly as possible.

Eve pulled over and eased the car into the next rest area. There were no other vehicles there. As soon as the car stopped, Dan exited slowly and stretched, still holding the manual. Eve followed him to a nearby bench, and the two sat beside each other.

"So, co-pilot, how much further to Eos?" Eve joked, trying to ease the tension.

"That's chief navigational officer, if you don't mind." Dan corrected her with a grin. "According to this map, I'd say we have about two hundred and fifty miles to go."

"Since you said 'we', I'm assuming you've given up on your plans to abandon me?" Eve asked hopefully.

"Well, I guess it would be better for both of us if we stuck together for a while. What have I got to lose? If they turn me away, then so be it. At least I can try and help you get there safely."

When Dan looked over to her, he found Eve staring directly at him.

"So, what's your ethnic background anyway?" she wondered, admiring his exotic features and dark complexion. "Are you Hispanic or Arabic or something like that?"

The question seemed to make him quite nervous.

"Uh...I'm a little of everything I guess..."

Eve thought he was being unusually vague, and sensed that he was hiding something. Maybe there was someone in the family tree that had done something bad, and he was ashamed of it. Whatever the reason, she didn't want to press any further right now. She graciously allowed him to change the subject when he opened the manual.

"So, this Eos place is quite elaborate, judging by these maps," Dan stated. "There's this cave or room, which is basically a library. Another is a medical clinic. There's a cafeteria, a gym, an indoor farm and so on."

"Yeah, I've read the whole manual a few times actually. There are also some bios in there about the caretakers of the various rooms. They're all fascinating and highly qualified people."

Dan nodded in agreement as he leafed through the pages. Eve pulled out a tube of sunscreen lotion. It was now afternoon and the sun was quite intense.

"Would you like some sunscreen," she offered.

"No, I'm fine. Thanks anyway."

"My fair Irish skin needs a lot of protection," Eve lamented.

"It's not like you're pasty white though, and you have perfect skin," Dan complimented her.

"Thanks, but you have no idea how many avocados were actually harmed during the making of this complexion."

Laughing at Eve's joke, Dan closed the book and stood up.

"Well, we better get some gas into your car."

After fueling up and using the bathrooms, which were luckily still open, they headed back out onto the open road.

***

Helen Delshay was in the kitchen, rustling through the contents of her deep freezer. The middle-aged woman was glad to find that its contents were still cold, some even partially frozen. She was planning to cook up a storm, once the power was restored. She would start with the more perishable items, such as the steaks, then work her way through the veggies. Just as she was closing the freezer, she was startled by a loud rap at the front door.

As soon as she opened the door, a flood of bright, Arizona afternoon sunlight invaded the living-room. And that's not all. Marilyn, the neighborhood gossip, entered with it. Without so much as a *hi* or *good afternoon,* she rushed in and started spouting away.

"You'll never guess what Judy just told me!"

"What is it?" Helen asked as she closed the door.

A concerned look instantly came to her face, as she feared the worst. Marilyn still had curlers in her hair. Whatever the news was, it obviously couldn't wait.

"Her husband just drove in from San Diego, where he was supposed to have a meeting..."

"Yes?" Helen said in anticipation.

"He says this power outage was caused by terrorists!"

"What?"

"Yeah!" continued Marilyn, "he says it's going to last indefinitely! They don't know how long it's going to be before they can fix it!"

Helen was well aware of Marilyn's ability to embellish and exaggerate. "Are you sure about this?"

"Yes, you can ask him for yourself if you don't believe me. Anyway, he says they still have power in San Diego, so he's taking his family there for a while. I say we should do the same!"

Helen wasn't sure how to respond to such a statement.

"How did terrorists knock out the power?" was her first thought.

"They used some kind of missile, and then someone hacked into the power grids on top of that!" Marilyn blurted.

"So, you mean there was no solar storm?"

"No, there really was one, apparently, that's how it all started, and then these wackos started taking advantage of the situation!"

"If this is true, then isn't there somewhere closer we could go to, instead of going all the way to the coast?" Helen asked.

"No, the closest areas with power are in California and along the Gulf coast. Arizona is completely shut down!"

"But I don't know anyone in San Diego," complained Helen.

"You know *me,* and I know San Diego really well. We could be roomies!" Marilyn said excitedly.

Helen didn't want to hurt her feelings, but she dreaded the very thought of living with Marilyn, even temporarily.

"I think I'll just tough it out here for a while. I have a lot of corn and other things ready to be harvested. I should be okay for a while."

"Well, how about this then?" proposed her older neighbor, if you do end up going there, we'll meet somewhere."

"How can we meet up, if we can't communicate?"

"Simple. I'll be at the entrance to Old Town State Park, at the corner of San Diego Avenue and Twiggs Street. I'll go there every Monday at noon, starting in October."

Helen agreed.

"Okay, that's a plan. In the meantime, I should start barbequing all my steaks before they get warm. Why don't you join me for dinner?"

"You don't have to twist my arm!" accepted the loud-talking Marilyn. "I'll go take these curlers out of my hair, and I'll be right back!"

***

The barren landscape of the New Mexican plains stretched out before the powder blue BMW, as Eve and Dan steadily made progress toward Eos.

"You know, it's like we're on the yellow brick road headed toward Emerald City, Dorothy," Dan joked.

"If I'm Dorothy, then who are you supposed to be? I know you're not cowardly, and you seem to have a good heart. That only leaves you with one other option," she smiled mischievously.

Dan smiled right back with a similar slyness.

"Well, how else would you explain my agreeing to come with you on this crazy trip?"

"Touché, scarecrow," Eve replied with a grin.

"That reminds me. Why is a sense of humor one of the assets for chosen ones?" Dan asked. "It seems kind of trivial."

"The main reason is so that everyone gets along with each other. And there are also some health benefits as well."

"How so?" Dan wondered.

"It's been proven scientifically that laughing releases good chemicals into your brain and nervous system, for one. It also tones certain muscles in your core," Eve pointed out.

Dan was becoming increasingly impressed with Eve's eclectic knowledge.

"Maybe, if the wizard gives me a brain, I'll be able to soak up random facts the way you do."

Eve couldn't help herself, as she kept the theme running along.

"With the thoughts you'll be thinkin', you could be another Lincoln..."

The pair exchanged very satisfied chuckles. Eve then concentrated on the curve ahead, as Dan stared out the window while breathing in the gentle scent from Eve's floral perfume.

"I don't mean to belittle you in anyway, but I was just curious..." Dan said.

"About?"

"I can understand why they would need exceptionally gifted people for this project, or whatever it is, but you seem like a pretty normal person. How exactly do you fit into all of this?"

"Oh yeah. I understand exactly where you're coming from. I asked Michael pretty much the same thing," Eve confessed. "You see nowadays, people with great technical skills are considered valuable. While those with more primitive abilities are considered outdated, and are less sought after. However, in the event of a technological breakdown, the opposite holds true. Even if you can build a supercomputer from spare parts, that's pretty useless, if there's no power to run it. On the other hand, if you know how to grow tomatoes for example, that could definitely come in handy. Most people today are so reliant on technology, they couldn't survive a week out in the wilderness with no gadgets. Yet that's how mankind survived, up until a relatively short time ago."

Dan nodded in agreement, as Eve continued.

"This may sound pretty trivial, but I know how to mend clothes and cook healthy food. And the last time I checked, most people still liked food and clothes."

Dan was genuinely curious to know more about his new friend.

"What other assets do you have?"

"Well, let's see," Eve thought. "I picked up management skills from running my family's jewellery stores, and I'm a registered dietician. That's one thing Michael noticed, when he hacked into my educational records."

"...Hold on a second," Dan interrupted. "You mean he broke the law? What happened to the big deal about honesty?"

Eve defended her mentor.

"You have to remember, if they make a mistake in choosing a candidate, it could jeopardize the whole endeavor. Also, they would never share any info about a candidate with anyone. Unless of course, it was a serious criminal matter."

"So, Michael's tech skills are valuable after all." Dan pointed out.

"Only for the selection process. After that, people with basic skills like you and me may be as valuable as the mentors and caretakers."

Dan was surprised by her assessment of him.

"How do you know I even have any basic skills? I mean, we just met yesterday."

Eve took a quick look at him.

"You said you live alone and your parents are gone. Yet you hold down a job, pay for an apartment, and you're well groomed. So, I can assume you're quite responsible."

"You shouldn't judge a book by its cover. But thanks for the compliments."

"You're very welcome," Eve said with a smile.

Dan suddenly noticed what appeared to be mountains manifesting in the distance.

"That should be Las Cruces up ahead, where those mountains are. We should make one more rest-stop before the final stretch," Dan suggested. "I hope there are some stores open too, so I can buy more water."

"You mean you only brought the one bottle with you?" Eve asked. "You're lucky I have air-conditioning."

"Yeah, I guess I wasn't thinking straight."

"I'll bet you brought your sports memorabilia with you though. Am I right?"

A guilty look came across Dan's face.

"Only a few baseball caps and one jersey," He declared, as Eve looked over to him with a smirk.

"Typical male pattern behaviour."

"Well, it is a Cowboys jersey after all. Is nothing sacred to you?" Dan protested, as he tried to keep a straight face.

"Yeah, I'm one to talk. I could be the poster girl for female yuppies."
"Why is that?"
"I'm all about the fashion, jewellery and beauty salons," Eve confessed.
"Come on, you can't be that shallow."
"Oh, but I am. Seriously, that's my flaw."
"I think your shallowness is only skin deep. Underneath that beautiful complexion, there's a beautiful heart too. After all, you *are* a chosen one, remember?"

Eve had been flattered by Dan's earlier compliments, but this one was special. She was emotionally touched by his observation.

"Thank you so much. That's probably the nicest thing anyone's ever said to me."

She felt as if Dan had seen right through her outer façade, right down to the real Eve.

"You're welcome," Dan responded with a warm smile.

"How about you? What's your weakness? If you even have one."

"Oh, I have many. Trust me. If I have to be honest, I would have to say low self-esteem is probably my biggest problem."

"Really? That certainly wasn't my first impression."

"Well, when I met you I was experiencing a bit of an adrenalin rush, so I wasn't quite myself. The truth is that I always feel insecure and out of place. I started working at the coffee shop with the intention of using it as a stepping stone. When I went for my first interview elsewhere, they practically laughed me out of the place. So, I've been at Zanetti's now for over four years, afraid to even try and better myself."

Dan sipped the last few drops of water from his plastic bottle.

"I mean it's a nice job and I am saving up a little bit for College, but I have no idea what field I even want to get into."

"I guess low self-esteem would explain why you don't have a girlfriend... I'm sorry, that sounded a bit insulting. What I mean is, I was wondering how you could possibly be unattached."

"Actually, I was wondering the same thing about you," Dan admitted.

"Well, you have to remember, I'm shallow and spoiled. I've had a few first dates, but I always end up finding faults with the guy. I guess I'm just too choosy. However, I am making a conscious effort to change my behaviour."

Eve let her statement sink in for a moment, before flashing a smile toward Dan. She hoped that he got the hint. Judging by the understanding grin on his face, she would have to assume that he did.

***

As Helen pulled into the supermarket parking lot, she noticed it was much busier than usual. Most of the shopping carts were also gone. Once inside, she knew it wasn't business as usual. She had never seen so many people in the store before. Luckily, she only needed a few items, mainly barbeque sauce and charcoal. Otherwise, this could take a while. If it was this busy because of a supposed temporary blackout, she thought to herself, what would it be like when everyone knew the true extent of it? She decided it would be wise to stock up on bottled water, and a few other staples, while she had the opportunity. She slowly made her way through the human traffic jam, toward the beverage aisle.

***

The official motto of Las Cruces is 'People helping people'. In this respect, Dan and Eve weren't disappointed. They had chanced upon a small restaurant that remained open, due to support from relatives and loyal customers. Some had brought their gas-grills, or plates and cutlery. Others had brought tortillas and beans, or corn from their own backyards. There was no menu service available, but there were enough burritos and enchiladas to satisfy all comers. There were about ten times as many people outside than could fit into the indoor dining area. By word of mouth alone, a spontaneous block party had somehow formed. Payment was by cash donations only, and an oversized jar had been set up for this purpose.

Dan and Eve's timing had been perfect. Dinner was just beginning when they pulled in. The unforeseen fiesta had given them a chance to practice their Spanglish, as well as helping restore Dan's faith in humanity.

"See," Dan said to Eve as he gnawed on a grilled cob of corn, "No one's fighting over mac and cheese."

"I sincerely hope I'm wrong, but I think it's a little early yet to make any judgements," Eve responded.

Dan digested that thought along with his dinner. Since a few curious crows had begun to loiter, Eve decided to be charitable. She shook her paper plate in their direction, catapulting half-kernels of corn and other morsels their way.

"They'll never leave you alone now," Dan said.

"That's okay, I don't mind. I kind of used to hate crows, I thought they were mean. Then I read about how intelligent they are, and their amazing survival skills, and I really admire them now. I know it's just my imagination, and I just never noticed them before, but they seem to follow me around."

"It's not your imagination," Dan countered, "did you notice that they're all on your side of the table? Maybe they've decided to make you their queen. I can't say I blame them," he said with some admiration of his own.

"Either that, or they're just afraid of you, scarecrow."

"You're really trying to make that nickname stick, aren't you?" Dan accused her.

"Perhaps you need to reinvent yourself. I have the perfect solution for you." Offered Eve.

"And just what might that be?" He asked hesitantly.

"Picture this – you open up a little place for them. You can call it, 'The Cawfe'. You'll be the world's first *crowbar*-ista," she teased with an almost straight face.

Dan tried not to smile, unsuccessfully.

"Hah-hah," he laughed mockingly. "Obviously, the *quality* of your sense of humor wasn't a factor for Michael. You just might get yourself unchosen, with that kind of material," he warned lightheartedly. "You really need to end this crow-themed obsession of yours."

"As you wish, my *raven*-haired friend."

"No! Stop!" Dan pleaded, although the glint in his eyes betrayed him. He was enjoying every minute of it, and they both knew it.

After dropping his last fifteen dollars in the jar and thanking everyone within earshot, Dan accompanied Eve back to the car. Their next stop was a nearby convenience store, where they were not met with the same hospitality. The bitter looking old clerk was charging ten dollars for a small bottle of water, citing the ancient law of supply and demand. Not that it mattered, as he would not honor Eve's personal cheques anyway. The two then decided to make one last sprint toward Eos, which by their estimate was about two hours away now. First however, Eve needed to get some more water out of the trunk. She popped it open and pulled out a medium sized blue cooler. Inside, there were a dozen bottles of ice-cold water. She pulled one out of the ice and threw it to Dan, who caught it happily.

"Thanks, I owe you one!"

"Actually, that'll be *five* dollars." Eve said.

"But it says one dollar right on the label," Dan protested.

"What are you whining about? That's half the going rate, so I hear." She shrugged her shoulders and grinned. "Supply and demand."

"Can I give you a verbal IOU?" Dan begged.

"I guess you're good for it," she said as she twisted off the cap from her own bottle. "Cheers!"

"Cheers!" Dan echoed, as he accepted Eve's toast and bumped her bottle.

**

About two hours later, they had nearly arrived at their destination. By now, Dan had his eyes firmly on the map, and was giving Eve instructions as to what to look for.

"It says to look for a big orange colored rock just before some really tall trees. There should be a dirt road between the two."

"There it is!" Eve said, just seconds later.

After turning onto the dirt-road, they only had to go about a half-mile, but the road surface was rough and Eve needed to go quite slow. After a few bumpy minutes, they had reached a cul-de-sac, where there were two other cars parked already. She pulled up behind a silver pick-up and turned off the engine.

After retrieving their suitcases, Dan led the way along a winding, rock-paved pathway to a high, stone wall. Behind the wall sat a very large home, which appeared to have strong adobe style influences. At the ornate wrought-iron gate they were met by cameras, and what appeared to be an intercom. Dan looked over to Eve and stated what they were both thinking.

"What if this whole thing is just some sort of elaborate joke...or worse?" Before Eve could open her mouth, a response came from a calm, booming male voice, through the intercom speaker apparently.

"I can assure you that this is all very real. Welcome to Eos, please state your names."

They were both rather startled, and began looking around uncomfortably. Eve moved forward to press the button on the intercom.

"You don't need to press the button, we can hear you fine. That's basically a prop for delivery people and such."

Eve realized the voice wasn't coming from the black box, but from a hidden speaker elsewhere.

"Uh...my name is Evelyn Donegan and... this is Daniel Goodrich."

After a few suspenseful moments of silence, the voice returned.

"Okay, I have your name here young lady, but could you repeat your name please, sir?"

Dan looked over to Eve nervously, and it was she who responded again.

"Actually, you won't find his name anywhere. He's not a chosen one." There was a short, but tense moment of silence, then the voice was heard again. It was still calm, but with a notable air of disappointment about it.

"Then why did you bring him here?"

"Because he saved my life! And he has the assets required to be a chosen one!" Eve rambled desperately.

The doorman wasn't buying it though.

"I'm sorry, but you're not a mentor. You don't have the training or the authority to choose candidates."

Dan then surprised everyone involved, with an unforeseen outburst.

"But we've come all this way to see the wizard! He's the only one who can help us!"

The man behind the stone curtain chuckled.

"At least you have a sense of humor..."

"...I know," Dan interrupted, "It's one of the assets, right?"

"Very good Dorothy...I mean Eve. You just may be mentor material," the unseen speaker replied. "However, allowing a non-chosen one into Eos would be a serious security risk. We have to consider the collective welfare of the community."

Dan didn't waste another second before speaking out.

"Look, she's a chosen one and I'm not. She stays, and I go. It's really quite simple."

Upon hearing this, Eve exploded.

"What?! There's no way I'm going in there alone and throwing you to the wolves! If you have to leave, then I'm coming with you!" And without so much as waiting for a response from Dan, or the hidden one, she picked up her suitcase and headed back. Dan did the same, and soon they were on the path, headed back toward the cul-de-sac.

"Wait! You can't leave!" Dan shouted uselessly, as he followed after her.

Chapter Four

Meet and Greet

Before they had reached the cul-de-sac, Eve noticed someone in the pathway coming toward them. She stopped to let Dan catch up to her. He immediately noticed the figure approaching as well, a slender male it seemed. As the man came closer, they could see he was a Native American. He appeared to be well into his sixties, with long, salt and pepper hair. Dan called out to the mystery man.

"Hello?"

"Good afternoon," he answered. "You two look lost."

He extended his right hand and introduced himself.

"My name is Qaletaqa."

"Nice to meet you. I'm Daniel, and this is Evelyn," Dan said as he accepted the stranger's hand. "We're not actually lost, we know where we are. How about you, are you visiting someone on this property?"

"Actually, I live in there," Qaletaqa said in a pleasant tone.

Dan and Eve looked at each other, each wondering what to ask next.

"Have you ever heard of Eos by any chance?" Dan asked hesitantly.

The man's face lit up a little.

"Of course, I was just making my way back there now. But why are you two going in the opposite direction?"

"They wouldn't let us enter," Dan said somberly.

The man's eyebrows bunched closer together.

"Why wouldn't they let you in?"

"It's because I'm not a chosen one," Dan confessed. "And she refuses to go in without me."

Qaletaqa looked at Eve, then at Dan, with a pensive stare.

"Are you okay?" Dan asked him.

After a few more awkward seconds, Qaletaqa spoke.

"Last night I had a dream. There was a man knocking on a door. I was on the other side and asked him who he was. But he answered: 'God is my judge.' I asked him again what his name was, but again all he said was: 'God is my judge.' I told him that only chosen ones may enter, but he only repeated the same words, without saying his name. And then the dream was over."

Dan looked over to Eve with a look that questioned the man's sanity. Eve understood the look perfectly. Dan then decided to humor their new acquaintance.

"Yeah, I've had some pretty freaky dreams myself. I'm sure it doesn't mean anything."

"Are you sure?" Qaletaqa asked curiously. "You did say your name is Daniel, did you not?"

"Yes, it is. But what does that have to do with your dreams?" Dan obviously wondered.

"You don't know the meaning of your name?" Qaletaqa asked him.

Dan thought about it for a second or two.

"I can't say that I do actually," he admitted.

The gentle looking man looked Dan square in the eyes.

"The name Daniel means 'God is my judge.'"

Neither Dan nor Eve knew how to respond to this surprise revelation, as Qaletaqa studied Dan's face a little closer.

"Do you have any Native American blood by any chance?" The stranger questioned Dan.

He answered with the same hesitancy as he did when Eve had questioned his ethnicity.

"Uh...I'm not sure. I suppose I could," he muttered.

Qaletaqa was not impressed.

"You sure don't know very much about yourself. That's not a good thing. However, you're obviously meant to be here at Eos," he stated rather casually.

Dan was practically in shock at this point.

"Are...are you sure?" he stammered.

"Well, you don't think I dream about strange men every night, do you?" Qaletaqa asked with a straight face, before bursting into hearty laughter.

Dan couldn't believe he might still be allowed in, but Qaletaqa's light heartedness had put him more at ease.

"Follow me," their new friend gestured.

"Are you sure you can get us in?" Eve asked, as the trio made their way back toward the house.

"Oh, I'm pretty sure I can. Unless they've all voted to kick me out of the club," Qaletaqa joked self-confidently.

Unbeknownst to the three, they were not alone. From a distance, a curious pair of eyes watched them from behind the trees. Human eyes...and it was no one associated with Eos. It wasn't the first time this visitor had spied on people as they entered or exited the property. Each time, whether by chance or design, he had managed to stay just beyond the reach of surveillance cameras.

When they reached the gate, they all stopped. Dan and Eve turned to Qaletaqa. He just stood there and waited. Within a second or two, the now familiar voice greeted them.

"*Welcome back Chief Q, I see you brought company.*"

"This is Evelyn and Daniel," Qaletaqa said as he gestured toward them.

"*Yes, we've met,*" the unseen man replied. "*But you do know he isn't a chosen one.*"

"Yes, I know he *wasn't*, but he is *now*," the Chief informed the gatekeeper.

"*You're the boss,*" the guard replied, as the heavy, iron gate slowly rolled to the right along it's track.

Dan looked at Eve and raised his eyebrows to let her know he was impressed. Apparently, they had just been allowed into Eos by the chief caretaker himself, by the sounds of it.

"Welcome to your new home," Qaletaqa said, as he led them along the wide driveway.

On either side of them lay perfectly landscaped lawns, flowerbeds, and various indigenous plants. When they reached the large, solid-wood front door, it opened immediately. They were greeted by a big man, wearing a sidearm. He was the head guardian at Eos and his name was Robert. The fifty-year old stood at six feet and three inches with short brown hair. He wore brownish camouflage, and was two hundred and thirty pounds of pure muscle, looking every bit a military man.

After being properly introduced to the newcomers, he escorted everyone through the house, toward the backyard. It was evident to Dan and Eve that whoever the owners of the house were, they must be quite wealthy. An oversized crystal chandelier hung in the living area. Tapestries adorned the walls, and rare vases and other antiquities decorated the luxury home. The handwoven Persian rug, which lay over the solid walnut floor, especially caught Eve's discerning eye.

Upon exiting through the back door, they were met with fruit trees and a large Italian water fountain. By this time, the sun was sitting very low in the sky. The muted evening light cast an idyllic glow over the pastel-brown colored home. The expansive property backed right up into the mountains of the Gila National Forest. When they reached the sloping grounds which led to the rocky terrain, Robert stopped, at what appeared to Dan and Eve to be a storm shelter. He lifted one side only of the large two door entrance, then gestured to the other three.

"Be my guest," he offered.

Qaletaqa led the way, followed by Eve, Dan and finally Robert, who closed the door behind him. They began their descent down the concrete stairway, which looked rather unnatural in its surroundings, and the two newest members simply could not believe their eyes. The underground cavern was massive, apparently as high as it was wide. Separating three long flights of stairs were lookout areas, all enclosed with wooden railings. Chief Q stopped at the highest one to act as a tour guide for his two speechless guests.

"This is one of the two main caverns. From the floor to the highest point is about four hundred feet," he informed them.

"You mean there's more to it than this?" Dan asked in astonishment.

"Oh yes. I would say this is probably about one third of it only," Chief Q added.

On the sprawling cavern floor below were partitioned areas, some of them open-air. The rooms which were covered were made of solid wood, while the uncovered areas were separated by stone walls, as in a castle. The entire setup looked like a cross between a lost city from an Indiana Jones movie, and a rustic country resort. Looking up, Dan and Eve could see sunlight streaming in from fissures in the ceiling. Although they didn't know it, these were manmade and strategically placed. There were small but powerful solar panels mounted on the walls of the cave, which feasted on this energy. There were also powerful looking lights attached about a quarter of the way up the walls, although they appeared to be only partially lit, at the moment. Dan noticed that the rooms directly underneath the fissures, were the ones with roofs, obviously to keep out any rain.

"Is that a forest?" Eve asked incredulously, as she pointed down toward the largest of the enclosures.

"Yes, it is. That's one of our sources of oxygen, along with the various gardens throughout the complex, mostly in the other main cavern," Robert answered her. "There's also an underground river which runs through one of the smaller caves."

"I didn't know trees could grow in caves," she said.

"Well, it is rare, but it's not the only place in the world with underground forests. Just a few years back, they discovered the Son Doong cave in Vietnam. It's similar to Eos, except it's completely natural, while most of the plant and animal life here was brought in."

"You mean there are animals in here as well?" Dan asked with a bit of astonishment.

"Yes, we had goats and chickens brought in for our resident farmer. We have some trained security dogs that work with our guardians as well, of which I'm the leader of."

"Who discovered this place?" Eve chimed in.

"I did actually," stated Chief Q. "Just like most of the caves in the world, it was by accident that I happened upon it. Although I had been led to this area by a dream, so in that sense, it wasn't an accident at all. You see, my ancestry is Mogollon and Hopi. The Mogollon lived in this area centuries ago, then supposedly vanished without a trace."

"Why supposedly?" Dan wondered.

"Well," pointed out Chief Q, "If they had indeed vanished, then I couldn't have Mogollon blood, could I?"

"How do you know you're a descendant?" Eve asked him.

"Because my daddy told me so." Chief Q said in an almost childlike way. "Most historians don't give oral tradition much credence, but with indigenous peoples, it's very important. I'm only guessing, but I think in times of strife they dispersed and mingled with other tribes. Some of them may have gone underground into places like this. We haven't done very much digging in here, nor do we want to, but I'll bet Archaeology would prove my theory. Especially since that's been the case with other caves in this part of the country. Then, when they re-emerged, they would also have blended in with nearby tribes. Regardless of the historical details, I strongly believe I was meant to find these caves, and use them for the same purpose.

Although, I feel the time has come to open it up to people from the four races."

"Four races?" Eve echoed.

"Red, yellow, black and white," Chief Q clarified.

"Oh, I see," Eve nodded.

However, Dan wanted to know more about Chief Q's assertion.

"How do you know you were meant to do this, Mister Kah…lay…taka?" he asked.

Chief Q smiled, as a parent does before answering their child's naïve questions.

"When you open your heart to the Great Spirit in prayer, he reveals things you could never know with your mind. And by the way, you can call me Chief Q, everyone does."

"I'm not sure if I believe in a Great Spirit though," Dan confessed. "Are you sure I really belong here?"

Chief Q chuckled again, as he was prone to do.

"That's okay. The Great Spirit obviously believes in you. Besides, we have a few agnostics here already. You'll fit right in. We also have Christians, Jews, Muslims and other religions represented here."

Dan seemed a little surprised by this revelation.

"Are you sure everyone will get along, even if they have different beliefs?" he said quite frankly.

Chief Q corrected him.

"I didn't say we had different beliefs, I only pointed out that we have different religions."

"There's a difference?" Dan asked bewilderedly.

"Oh yes!" Chief Q declared emphatically. "Everyone here believes in good. How about you my friend? Do you believe in good, or evil?"

"Well, *good* of course!" Dan responded eagerly.

"Then good," said the wise elder. "I rest my case. Just remember this quote from Chief Tecumseh; 'Trouble no one about their religion. Respect theirs, and demand that they respect yours.'"

Dan and Eve weren't sure who this Chief Tecumseh was, but they gave their new leader affirmation with their facial expressions and nods. At this point, Robert excused himself to attend to other duties. And with that, Chief Q headed down the second flight of steps.

"Follow me, I'll show you to your dwellings," he said.

Eve and Dan followed closely behind.

"I don't know about you, but to me dwelling sounds like code for tent, or hole in the wall," Dan said to Eve quietly.

"I hope not. I'm not the camping type," she responded.

The Chief could overhear their conversation and tried to reassure them.

"Oh, I think you'll be pleasantly surprised."

There was a main pathway made of paving stones, which connected the entire complex. As the three made their way from the first cavern to the second, Dan and Eve looked around in awe. They still couldn't believe this whole other world existed underneath their own.

"When you have time, make sure you take that self-guided tour that's in the manual," Chief Q said.

They then passed through a narrower, tunnel-like arca leading to the next cavern, which was the dwelling area of Eos. When they entered it, Dan and Eve were pleasantly surprised, just as Chief Q had predicted. The floor area was made up of stone-walled enclosures, most of these without ceilings. However, instead of working quarters, these were gardens. Some came complete with ponds, butterflies, and ladybugs.

What really amazed the young pair however, were the wooden apartment-like terraced walls of the cavern. There were hundreds of these little homes clinging to the sides of the cave. They were very rugged and sturdy looking log cabins, set up in such a way as to support each other, much like stairs. At the same time, the entire structure was also wedged perfectly into the rock walls, for extra support. The very bottom homes were built on top of massive upright logs, which were the foundation of the entire set-up. Accessibility to each home worked exactly like the seating in movie theatres, with steps leading up to a row of abodes, and then a pathway in front.

"This entire place must have cost a fortune to build," Dan stated with utter amazement.

"Yes, but I was fortunate to have a billionaire on board very early into the planning stages," said Chief Q. "On your left is where the ladies live. Gentlemen are on the right, and couples on the far wall. There are a good number of bathrooms with showers. These are spread out evenly and marked with big signs, so you should have no trouble finding them."

The Chief then took the path leading to the left side, so clearly, they were making their way to Eve's new pad. From the looks of it, most of the dwellings were still vacant.

"It's first come, first serve, so feel free to choose any available dwelling. If there is no curtain in the window, then it's still available. They're all about the same distance to the bathrooms and the cafeteria down below. Which reminds me," he said to Eve, "I believe you were going to be working there, correct?"

"Yes, I'm the dietician. I'll be creating the menus," she said with a smile.

"And we'll have to find *you* some employment as well," Chief Q said to Dan. "I'm thinking you should train to be a guardian."

Dan felt a little overwhelmed, to say the least.

"Me...a guardian? I don't have any security or military background whatsoever."

"It's true I don't know very much about you son, but I truly feel in my heart that's where your calling is," Chief Q overruled.

"...I'll take this one!" Eve suddenly blurted out, pointing to a dwelling.

It was about one hundred and fifty square feet in size, as were all of them. They basically consisted of a bunk, a table, and a small living area with drawers built into the walls. The only entry was through a small front door, and there were two windows on each side of the door. The sides were shared walls with the neighboring abodes. Eve entered her chosen piece of real estate, and set down her suitcase.

"As you can see," pointed out Chief Q, "We only used cedar. That's because it's mold resistant, as well as durable."

Dan poked his head inside and took a peek.

"Cool! This whole set-up is better than Batman's cave," he said enthusiastically.

"Well, we'll leave you alone to settle into your new home. If you need any help, just ask a neighbor. And if they can't help you, there's an intercom which connects you to the guardians. They also double as customer service reps," Chief Q stated with a grin. "You'll find enough food in there for a couple of days, until we get set up properly. You can report to the cafeteria tomorrow morning at your leisure, to meet with the cooks."

"What about my car?" Eve wondered. "Do you think it'll be fine where it is?"

"Oh, that's right! I almost forgot. A guardian will take it and put it in our hidden underground parking lot. I'll need to get your car keys for that."

As Chief Q received Eve's spare keys, he dismissed himself from her abode.

"Okay then. Have yourself a good night, Miss Donegan."

"Good night everyone!" Eve said to them as she closed the door.

Chief Q turned to Dan.

"And now, it's your turn to go house hunting."

"Is there any way for Eve and me to communicate with each other?" Dan asked.

"Yes. It's called talking," Chief Q joked. "No, I'm afraid the living quarters are not quite that sophisticated."

Dan waved off the issue with his right hand.

"Not a problem. If she's in charge of the food, I'll find her."

He then smiled at Eve and the two exchanged 'good nights.'

"Thanks for everything, by the way," Dan added.

"It was really my pleasure," Eve replied with a coy smile.

When Chief Q and Dan reached the opposite side of the cavern, Dan chose a suite directly across from Eve's.

"By the way, there's a hand-crank emergency lamp in all the dwellings," the elder leader informed his guest. "In case the power goes off at night. We run on a combination of wind and solar power, with a backup diesel generator. It's worked fine so far, but once we have a full house, it could be a problem."

"Great," said Dan. "By the way, do you have any extra manuals handy? Since I didn't have a mentor, I never got one."

"Oh, certainly, I'll bring you one in a little while. You'll need those maps especially."

Once chief Q had left, Dan settled into his new home. He sat down on the bunk to test it out, and was quite surprised at the level of comfort. On top of the table was a large gift basket without wrapping, just a bow. It consisted of beef jerky, various nuts, dried fruits, crackers, juices, and other non-perishable foods. On the floor, beside the table, was a small water cooler. After finding a cup in one of the cupboards, Dan had a refreshing drink of the cool water, before heading to the suitcase to unpack. It took him roughly half an hour to put everything away.

A few moments later, Chief Q returned right on cue with the manual. Dan lay down on his bunk and leafed through the booklet, until he got to the page with the tap code chart. While he was studying it, he noticed that the lighting outside had increased its intensity. This gave Dan an idea. He grabbed a small pair of binoculars which he'd packed, went over to the left window, and searched for Eve's place across the cavern. At first, he wasn't quite sure which one it was. But while scanning the general area where he thought it was, he glimpsed Eve through her still uncovered window. He quickly went back to the bed and grabbed the manual, as well as the emergency lantern off the floor. Using the tap code chart, he sent signals in Eve's direction. He aimed the light to her window, and turned it on and off with the required pauses in between. He did it with his right hand, while trying to guide it with the binoculars in his left hand. It would have been far more noticeable had it been darker in the cave, but his persistence finally paid off.

After repeatedly signalling 'Hi Eve,' a light started to flash from the other side. The response was 'Hi Dan,' not surprisingly. Dan followed up with 'Good night.' He then wrote down the numbers she had signalled him, and after looking those up in the chart, found that they spelled out 'Sweet dreams.' He couldn't help but smile proudly with a sense of accomplishment. He had successfully communicated with her across the cavern, without the aid of modern technology. Dan felt like a kid playing in a treehouse. He went to bed reviewing the entire day's happenings, as he tried to get accustomed to his new environment. Meanwhile, his jacket lay draped over a chair by the table, the still unopened letter sticking out of the chest pocket.

Over on the opposing wall, Eve also retired for the evening, obsessing over how romantic it was of Dan to send her coded messages.

***

After Helen and Marilyn had finished their barbeque dinner and cleaned up, they said their farewells to one another. As her guest flicked on her flashlight and turned towards the pitch-black darkness, Helen closed and locked the front door. She then looked over to the portrait of her departed husband William, which dominated the fireplace mantle. It was surrounded by smaller photos and military medals and awards.

"Well, looks like we're alone at last dear."

Chapter Five

The Nesting Stage

On his first morning at Eos, Dan awoke to soft shafts of filtered light leaking through the window shades. He wasn't sure exactly what time it was. The night before, he had been too tired to look for an outlet for his clock. He picked up the manual and turned to the floor plan, before letting out a long drawn out yawn and walking over to the window groggily. Down below, Dan could see exactly where the bathroom facilities were, as well as the cafeteria. These would be the starting points of his self-guided tour.

In fact, it was already ten o'clock in the morning and Eve was already in the cafeteria, which is where Dan bumped into her after taking a shower. She was sitting at a table with a fellow dressed as a chef, and there was one other person in the room, an elderly gent sitting alone sipping coffee. When Dan entered, he bade good morning to the solitary man as he walked by. Eve heard their exchange and turned around immediately.

"Good morning, sleepy head!"

"Good morning, Eve," Dan responded with a smile. "I guess I'm too late for breakfast and too early for lunch?"

Eve and the chef stood up.

"Dan, this is Chef Steven," Eve said as she introduced her co-worker.

"Nice to meet you sir," Dan politely addressed him as they shared a handshake.

"Nice to meet you too, but you must call me Steven or Steve, or even chef. 'Sir' makes me feel old."

"Okay, Chef Steven it is then," Dan concluded.

"I'll tell you what. There's still some left-over bacon and hash browns I can warm up. How do you like your eggs?" Inquired Chef Steven.

"Oh, um...over easy would be great. Thank you so much," Dan said hungrily.

"No problem, that's what I'm here for."

As the chef left, Dan and Eve sat down across from each other.

"You better enjoy that bacon while you can," Eve notified him."

"Uh oh, are you going to make us follow a strict, healthy diet?"

"It's not so much that. Bacon and a lot of other foods are in short supply around here. Once they run out, Chef Steven and I are going to have to become a little creative," Eve stated frankly.

"Well, anything beats having to stand in a bread line, or whatever it is that's going to happen back home," Dan shrugged.

"It's actually quite amazing just how well equipped this place is though," said Eve. "The kitchen is restaurant calibre, and a lot better engineered. The heat and steam produced from cooking is filtered, then recycled into the heating system. Chef Steven said they manage to keep all of Eos at or near room temperature, year-round."

"Yeah, after I eat I'm going to take a look around for myself," Dan divulged. "I'm not sure how many people are still to come, but I only met one guy in the bathroom area just now."

Eve looked at Dan like a mother looks at a child when she's unimpressed with their behaviour.

"That's because you slept in. I met a whole bunch of ladies when I went for my shower at seven-thirty."

"Okay, I get the hint," Dan smiled. "I'll have to make sure to set my alarm tonight."

Eve quickly changed the subject. Looking down at her clipboard, she grinned coyly.

"That was pretty cool, what you did with the light signals last night," she recalled.

Dan looked straight at her, waiting for her to look up. As soon as she did, their eyes met and Dan responded simply;

"Thanks."

They continued to stare at each other, until it became awkward. Dan felt that he should break the silence, before it became downright embarrassing.

"Would you be interested in joining me for the grand tour?"

"Oh, I really wish I could…" she said with genuine disappointment, "but I have to make a menu for Chef Steven. This is a lot more complicated than I expected. We have to provide Vegan, Halal, and Kosher options. Not to mention working around food allergies. I'll be here at seven for dinner though. There are three serving times for each meal, because there's only five of us working in the kitchen, and the seating is limited of course. If you sign up for seven o'clock, we can have dinner together every night," she suggested hopefully.

"Sounds great, where do I sign up?" Dan asked.

"In that book over there," Eve said, pointing to a wooden stand by the entrance. "There are a whole bunch of slots still open. The six o'clock serving time is already filled, not surprisingly."

Dan went over to the book, signed it, and returned to the table.

"There, it's a date! Well…you know what I mean," he added nervously.

Eve's only response was to giggle and smile.

Suddenly, Chef Steven popped out from the kitchen carrying a tray. "Here you go. Bon appétit! Coffee, tea, and juice are on that table over there. Help yourself," Chef Steven offered.

"Thanks," Dan said as he eyed the generous portions.

While Dan enjoyed his meal, Eve continued writing notes on her clipboard, in between little bits of chit chat. Afterwards, Dan excused himself.

"Well, I better leave you to your work now. See you at dinner."

Eve waved him off with a smile.

"Be there or be hungry!" she advised him.

It took Dan only about five minutes to make his way from the cafeteria to the other cavern. He decided he would visit the agricultural enclosures first. The walls were made of solid wooden logs. He noticed the front door here was a lot bigger than all the ones he'd seen previously. He pushed the doorbell and waited. He hoped he wasn't interrupting any important work. He decided that if no one came soon, he shouldn't try again.

Just before Dan was about to turn and leave, he heard the door creaking open. He was greeted by a slim yet sturdy looking man of above average height, who appeared to be in his late forties to early fifties, and clean shaven.

"Howdy partner! Come on in. You must be Tim, the trainee I've been expecting."

"Uh...actually my name is Dan. I'm just here to get acquainted with Eos, and the people who run it. I hope I didn't come at a bad time."

"Not at all! The only bad time would be if I was sleepin'" the man said with a strong Texan accent. "My name is Willie, nice to meet you Danny boy!" he said, as he shook Dan's hand firmly.

"There're some boots over yonder. You should change out of them runnin' shoes, it's a little dirty round here. This *is* a farm after all."

Dan looked around as he walked over to the side shelving where the boots were. This was the biggest enclosure on the map, and he could see why. It seemed that this was where they grew most of their food and housed the animals. Dan changed his footwear and caught up with Willie, who was feeding alfalfa hay to the goats.

"Is that their main diet?" Dan asked.

"This, and any greenery basically. Although we'll be giving them mostly pellets later, once our hay supply runs out. Have you ever milked a goat?" the rugged farmer asked with a grin.

"Actually...I've never milked anything," Dan admitted.

"Well, watch how I do it. Then you can try."

Once Dan had completed his introductory course in goat milking, and quite successfully at that, Willie led his guest to the chicken coops.

"We've got enough chicken feed to last about four months. They eat a lot less than goats, as you could probably guess. After that we can give them scraps, if need be. We also recycle eggshells for them. We wash 'em, dry 'em and crush 'em, then feed them back to the hens for calcium. The roosters need even less nutrients than hens because they don't lay eggs."

"How often *do* they lay eggs by the way?" Dan wondered.

"Once a day! And you thought humans had it rough," Willie quipped. "And if you're ever on egg duty, make sure you discard any eggs with cracks in 'em, however slight."

"Why's that?"

"Coz they could have salmonella. It's very common for poultry to carry the disease, and it could get into the eggs through cracks. Also, make sure you always wash your hands after touching poultry or going anywhere near their surroundin's," warned farmer Willie.

Dan was finding this all very educational, and was genuinely looking forward to learning more about basic farming.

As the two were leaving the animals behind and walking toward the produce area, Dan noticed beams of sunlight hitting the rows of tomatoes.

"I assume those openings in the ceiling were strategically placed?"

"That's right, and if you'll notice, we also have those lamps along the sides. These are turned on a few hours a day as needed, to assist with the light requirements."

"What are those watery contraptions over there?" Dan asked, pointing at a tiered area made of glass and wood.

Water was cascading from one level to another, then recycling itself.

"We grow lettuce and beans in that thing using just light and water. It was engineered by Professor Richards, who used to work for NASA. The man's a genius in my opinion."

"I guess soil is a limited commodity inside a cave," Dan reasoned.

"Actually, that's not the main concern," said Willie. "I mean, they purdy much could have shipped in enough soil to fill this whole area. The thing is, once the nutrients in the soil are used up, it takes more time and labor to enrich it again. So, we used the soil for bigger plants, trees, and shrubs."

"Are you sure you can produce enough food for all of us indefinitely?" Dan worried.

"Don't forget we also have a fish farm by the river, at the other end of the caverns, in addition to all the things we planted on the outside. Of course, we had to take the varying altitudes of the terrain into consideration. Somethin' that might do well at this level, would die at a higher or lower altitude. We get a good supply of Agave syrup from down in the desert area, by the way."

"It's amazing how well planned out and efficient Eos is!" Dan exclaimed.

"And nothin' goes to waste here my friend," Willie added. "You see those lettuce and celery stalks there in the water. Those came from the cafeteria."

"You mean you can grow those into actual celery and lettuces?"

Dan's curiosity had been piqued, and farmer Willie couldn't help but laugh.

"The only things you city folk seem to know about is high-tech gadgets and such. Yeah, there're all sorts of stalks and shoots you can grow in just a bowl of water."

Dan was fascinated by this quirky Texan character. He spent the next hour asking as many questions as he could, before moving on to his next planned stop, which was the library.

***

On a typical Friday afternoon, Helen would often invite a neighbor over for tea or coffee. She would even call on Marilyn occasionally, as a last resort of course. However, it seemed all her neighbors had decided to head for greener pastures, as no one answered her calls. The few people she did see who were still in the area, were either complete strangers, or barely acquaintances. So, she decided to venture out into the backyard instead, and pick some fresh corn to go with her barbeque dinner.

As she fetched a basket and her oversized hat, she wondered how long she could use the grill before she ran out of propane. Fortunately, she had been able to add to her already substantial charcoal supply the day before. If this power outage lasted much longer, she could still do it the old-fashioned way, for a while at least.

As she made her way through the rows of corn, she wondered if she wasn't becoming a little senile. Being only forty-two years old, this wasn't a possibility she had previously considered.

"I could swear I had seen some corn here still," she thought out loud.

As she passed from one stalk to another and combed through the leaves meticulously, she began to feel a knot tighten in her stomach. Nothing. Not a single ear. How could this be? Two days ago, about half the crop remained. When she had reached the end of her modest garden, a dumbfounded Helen stopped and looked around. Not just at her garden, but at the entire neighborhood in general. She was a trusting, good natured person, but she couldn't help feeling angry and personally violated. She just stood there with her empty basket, frowning sadly.

***

Immediately upon entering the library, Dan noticed a mature and sophisticated woman inserting books into the shelves. She turned and greeted him as soon as she glimpsed him in the corner of her eye.

"Hello. Welcome to the Eos public library," she said playfully.

"Hi. According to the manual, you must be Miss Jenkins," Dan deduced.

"The one and only, and in the flesh," she grinned.

"It says here you have master's degrees in history and literature," Dan said with admiration.

"Yes, I must admit I'm probably overqualified for my current position," she joked. "But it does have its benefits though, like survival for example."

"So, what kind of books would I find here?" Dan asked.

"Well, I'm afraid you won't find any romance novels, if that's what you're looking for," she teased, as Dan chuckled. "Ninety percent of these books are non-fiction; mostly atlases, dictionaries, religious texts, health references and so on. The fiction selection consists mainly of classic literature and poetry. In other words, you may not find what you want, but you'll probably find what you need."

"Makes sense," Dan reasoned.

"In addition to books, we also have a catalogue of seeds. You see, the humidity in here is perfectly regulated. Since humidity adversely affects both books and seeds, it makes sense to house them together."

The svelte older woman with glasses then gestured toward five large filing cabinets.

"We have three categories; indigenous, domestic and foreign. Indigenous covers the species you would find in this area. Domestic would be species found in the continental U.S., and foreign would cover tropical rainforests and such. They're kept in custom made, vacuum-sealed packets, designed to keep out light, heat and moisture. They should remain viable for decades."

"And what kind of seeds are they?" Would it be like fruits and vegetables, or flowers and plants?" Dan asked her.

"Oh, anything and everything we could get our hands on; trees, shrubs, fruits, flowers, vegetables…of course it's not a comprehensive collection, like the doomsday vault."

"What's the doomsday vault?" Dan wondered curiously.

"Oh, that's in Norway. They have a collection of almost every seed known to man. It's basically a Noah's Ark of seeds," She clarified.

"That sounds very useful," Dan nodded, before asking if he could browse through the library for a while.

Miss Jenkins was more than happy to show him around. At about four in the afternoon, Dan decided he should move along, if he was going to complete his itinerary. His last stop for the day would be the fitness room.

After a minute's walk from the library, he arrived there to find the door wide open. There were two people inside. One was a middle-aged, fit looking Indian fellow dressed in grey exercise garb with a light blue turban. The other was an older fellow dressed more like a tourist than anything else. The moment Dan walked in, he was greeted by the gym's caretaker.

"Good afternoon. Welcome, my friend," he said with a thick Indian accent. "My name is Ranjit, and what are *you* called please?"

"Oh, my name is Dan. Nice to meet you," he said, as he stuck out his right hand.

Ranjit met him halfway across the floor and accepted it.

"Congratulations! You are being our fourth customer today, and the first thousand customers get a free lifetime membership!"

"I thought there would only be about half that number in total at Eos," Dan said with a suspicious grin.

"Yes, yes, that is true. I just wanted to make you feel like a winner. Plus, everyone is loving a bargain, no?"

"I can't argue with that," Dan conceded, as Ranjit gestured toward the other gentleman, who had just begun his bike trip to nowhere.

"This is one of your new neighbors, Edward."

The man got off the machine and shook Dan's hand.

"Nice to meet you Dan."

"Likewise," Dan responded with a smile.

The fitness room wasn't very large and held only seven different machines, but it had another important function besides exercise.

"Would you be liking to join Edward and me in supplying energy to the Eos power-grid?" Ranjit inquired of Dan.

"What do you mean exactly?" asked a bewildered Dan.

"You see, each of these machines is connected to the power room next door. Whenever we exercise, we are also charging some batteries." Ranjit informed him proudly.

Dan had now come to expect such efficiency.

"Sure, it would be my pleasure. I could use a little unwinding, after the stressful past couple of days."

He and Ed hopped on the two bikes, while Ranjit took to the treadmill. Ed, who was by far the eldest, broke a sweat within moments. Ranjit and Dan were still quite fresh and energetic when the intercom sounded.

"Attention please! Could Daniel Goodrich please come to the security room at the earliest convenience! Repeat, could Daniel Goodrich please come to the security room at the earliest convenience! Thank you!"

"Looks like you're being called to the principal's office," joked Ed.

"Yeah, maybe they realize they made a mistake in allowing me to stay here," Dan said half seriously. "Well, it's been a quick pleasure my friends. I'll have to charge those batteries later I'm afraid. I have a dinner date tonight, and I don't want to be late."

"Ooh..." Ed and Ranjit teased in sync, as Dan waved to them while exiting.

On his way out the door, Dan peeked at the manual. The security room was located near the entrance, beside a stairway.

He had never visited Europe, but the stone-paved paths around Eos reminded Dan of the cobblestone streets he'd seen in movies. The beams of sunlight emanating from the fissures in the cavern ceiling, still provided most of the lighting, even this late in the afternoon. Their task aided only by a few lights here and there. Looking up, he noticed for the first time how the solar panels were set up. They were mounted halfway up the walls at the north, east, and west sides. Although Dan didn't know it, shafts of light were always hitting at least one panel throughout the daylight hours.

On his walk to the security room he also noticed two windmills, placed about two thirds of the way up the cavern walls. These also were strategically placed, so as to catch the draft for energy, while also helping to ventilate the cavern.

Before he reached his target, he could already see two figures standing outside the entrance. As he approached, he could make out two men wearing the guardian's uniform of brown and olive green camo. They had been busy talking to each other, but as soon as they caught sight of Dan, they turned their attention to him. Waving, one of them called out to him.

"Hi Dan, how's it going?"

"Oh, hi Robert!" Dan answered with a smile.

Beside Robert was a younger, blond fellow of average height and weight. For some reason, Dan felt he had the look of a used car salesman.

"Glad to meet your acquaintance Dan, my name is Chad."

After the usual round of handshaking and small talk, Robert invited Dan inside. The trio made themselves as comfy as they could, considering they only had wooden chairs at their disposal.

"So, Chief Q tells me you're our last-minute trainee," disclosed Robert.

"Really? I thought he was just kidding when he said that," conveyed a somewhat surprised Dan.

"Did he crack up like a kindergartner laughing at a cheesy joke afterwards?" inquired Chad.

"No actually, he didn't," Dan conceded.

"Then he was being serious," concluded Robert.

The two guardians nodded at each other in agreement.

"So, are you up for it?" Chad solicited.

Dan answered with visible hesitancy.

"Well...I'm not sure I have the qualifications...but I *am* willing to give it a try."

"Great. The job is yours," approved Robert. "Chief Q obviously thinks you've got the right stuff, and as far as the skills required...we can take care of that aspect of it. Can you start tomorrow morning?"

"Sure. Unless I get a better job offer," Dan quipped.

"Awesome!" Robert rejoiced as he arose from his seat. "Be here at nine o'clock in the morning and we'll get you started."

Dan agreed, as he and Chad also stood up. The two guardians then went back to their duties, and Dan headed back to his new apartment to groom himself for dinner.

When Dan entered the cafeteria about an hour later, Eve was serving at a table near the back. Unlike at his late breakfast earlier, the room was basically full, mostly with new faces. Although he did recognize a few of the people he'd met earlier that day, and made some small talk with them. As soon as Eve glimpsed Dan, she looked up at the clock. She then removed her apron and met him halfway across the floor.

"Hi there. You're right on time." She lilted.

"If there's one thing in this world I'm never late for, it's dinner," Dan assured her.

Eve looked around and found a table with two vacant spaces.

"I guess we can sit over here...excuse me, are these seats taken?" she inquired of the foursome.

"No. Make yourselves comfy," responded the smiling Asian lady in a red sweater.

Dan and Eve thanked them as they sat down, then introduced themselves. The Asian lady was Susan. Her husband was Ken.

The older couple seated across from them were Jack and Marie, from Ohio. Dan and Eve took a seat across from each other.

"So, are you two married?" Marie blurted out of the blue.

"Oh no, we're just friends," Eve announced immediately.

"Yeah, we just met yesterday," Dan quickly added.

"I'm sorry," Jack apologized. "You'll have to excuse my wife, she's socially handicapped. She'll just say whatever pops into her pretty little head."

"Well, it's just that they look so happy together," Marie claimed in her own defense.

"Then you know they can't be married!" her husband joked.

Everyone at the table enjoyed a hearty laugh. Although Dan and Eve seemed a bit embarrassed by the whole issue.

Dinner was served a few moments later. After dinner was finished and the table had been cleared, everyone stayed and got to know each other better.

Ken was a dentist and informed everyone at the table that, if they needed his services, they should look for him at the clinic. Susan was a nurse, and so the two would be working together there. Marie was retired, as was her husband Jack, who shared some of his military stories with the rest of them. Everyone was especially impressed with his work in Vietnam as a landmine diffuser. Marie had been a housewife for most of her life, but she did have a degree in counselling. She had worked in a high school for a few years before marrying Jack and raising four kids. Her counselling experience had come in very handy, according to her husband.

After about an hour, Jack and Marie excused themselves.

"Well, we better head off now, it's almost our bedtime," said the ex-sergeant. "Good night everyone."

"Good night!" everyone echoed.

"They're such a nice couple," said Susan. "I hope we can all return home soon, this must be really hard on them."

"It's hard on everyone, to just leave your life behind, but I guess we should count our blessings," Ken opined.

"Definitely," Dan agreed. "We pretty much have everything we need here. Chief Q and the others have done an amazing job."

"Don't get me wrong," said Eve. "I'm grateful for everything they're doing here. I just think they could have found some space somewhere for a spa, or at least a little beauty salon."

"Amen, sister!" Susan agreed, as the two fellows just grinned at each other.

Susan then elbowed Ken in the side and stood up.

"We should be running along now too," she winked at her husband, who immediately understood and followed suit.

"It was really nice meeting you both," Ken announced.

After they had all exchanged their farewells, a sudden awkward silence descended over the table. Dan seemed a little nervous with the idea of being alone with Eve. Sensing this, she helped him out by breaking the silence.

"So, how was your self-guided tour?"

"Oh, it was awesome. I learned so much in just one day. If you ever have a goat you need milked, I'm your man."

"That's good to know," Eve giggled.

"And how was your day?" Dan inquired. "Is Chef Steven treating you well?"

"Oh, he's just a sweetheart. He's a little eccentric, but very sociable, and a very skilled chef. By the way, I heard your name over the loudspeaker this afternoon. What was that all about?" Eve asked curiously.

"That's what I was going to tell you. You're looking at the newest guardian. I report for training in the morning."

"Wow, that's great!" beamed Eve. "I think you'll make a great guardian!"

"That's what everyone seems to think, for some reason. I guess we'll find out soon enough," Dan reasoned. "So, how are you adjusting to your new surroundings? Do you miss your friends?"

"Well, of course. And I miss my pampered lifestyle," confessed Eve. "I'm just a spoiled brat, you know."

"No. Spoiled...yes, but definitely not a brat." Dan offered with a consoling smile.

Eve smiled back before her facial expression took a more serious turn. "I wonder what it's like back home. I wish we had some news."

"Actually, Robert says there's a guardian out surveying the situation. He should be back in a few days."

"Do you miss your friends too?" Eve asked as she leaned in closer to Dan's side of the table.

"To be honest, I don't really miss their company. Being with everyone here at Eos, including you, has made me see what an immature bunch I hang out with. But I do worry about them. I hope they're all doing okay back home."

"I try not to worry," said Eve, "I just keep them in my prayers every night. It's something I've been in the habit of doing since I was a little girl. You're going to think I'm silly, but I even pray for my fish. As if God cares about my dumb little fishies."

"I don't see why he wouldn't. If God went to the trouble of imagining them and creating them in the first place, why wouldn't he care about them afterwards?" Dan reasoned.

"Good point," Eve agreed. "You know, for an agnostic, you're quite spiritual."

"To tell you the truth, I surprise myself sometimes," Dan confided. "Of course, it's all irrelevant now, my fishies are all doomed. I just hope they don't suffer too much."

On that note, the conversation dried up, and the two found themselves gazing into each other's eyes.

"Thanks for bringing me here," Dan relayed, in a suddenly softer voice.

"You're very welcome," Eve assured him as she kept eye contact.

"I guess it's time for us to call it a night as well," Dan imparted. "Would you like me to walk you to your hole in the wall?"

"Thanks for offering, but I have to talk with the chef about tomorrow's menu first," she lamented. "At what time are you having breakfast?"

"I have to be at the security room at nine, so I guess I'll be coming here at seven every morning. How about you?"

"I'll be helping till eight. So, I guess I'll be serving you breakfast from now on," Eve declared with delight.

"Great! I like my bacon crispy," he teased.

"Sorry mister! From now on we're going to be eating a lot healthier around here," she fired back.

As Dan arose from the table, he bid her good night.

"See you in the morning," Eve bubbled. "Sweet dreams,"

Dan was still a few feet away when he suddenly stopped, and turned halfway.

"Oh, and for the record...a beauty salon is the last thing you need," he professed shyly, before turning back and walking away.

Eve planted her left elbow on the table, and rested her head on the palm of her hand. With a content but distant look on her face, she processed Dan's parting compliment, as well as his recent behaviour in general. She could have little doubt that he felt the same way about her, as she did about him.

Chapter Six

First Day on the Job

"So, what's your favorite flavor of tree?" Robert inquired.

"Favorite flavor?" Dan repeated with a puzzled look.

"Yeah. First thing you gotta learn is basic survival skills," he pronounced assertively as he held down a tree branch for his companions.

Chad was following close behind as they made their way out of a canyon, inside the Gila National Forest.

"Ponderosa pine is my personal fave," Chad volunteered.

"Excellent choice," Robert agreed. And the seeds are big and easy to remove from the cones. Pinyon are also a great source of Pine nuts."

"Oh. I like Pine nuts," Dan contended. "Is that what you meant? Favorite kind of nut?"

"No. I meant actual trees," Robert insisted.

"You can eat trees?" Dan asked in bewilderment.

"Well, not the entire tree, and not all species," Robert clarified. "You can't eat the outside bark, but right underneath are two edible layers. I'll show you how to get at it when we reach that stand of Pinyon up ahead. You can eat it raw or boil it, but it's not very tasty either way. I like it pan-fried with butter, and salted."

It was eleven-thirty in the morning and the sun was quickly warming things up, as it normally does in this sunny part of the country. When they had reached the forested area above the canyon, Robert went up to one of the trees. He pulled out a very sturdy looking metal-handled knife from his pack. With a single overhanded swing, he thrust the blade forcefully into the trunk. He then cut the bark downwards about eight inches, using a forward and back jinking motion.

"You don't want to cut off more than about an eighth of the circumference. In fact, even that could potentially kill a tree. So, you should only do this in an emergency. The best thing to do is to find a branch that has broken off, then you can harvest the entire limb."

After removing the blade, he cut a similar parallel line about seven inches to the left. Two more horizontal incisions completed the rectangle. He then peeled off the piece of bark and showed it to his trainee.

"That light colored layer right here is what you're looking for. It's the living part of the tree."

Robert then pointed to the liquid oozing out of the bare patch of trunk.

And that's like its blood. It has a high sugar content, so it's great for some quick energy."

"Is that resin?" Dan wondered aloud.

"Oh no, resin is more like the waste. It's what they use to make turpentine. This is the sap."

"What if I confuse the two," Dan worried.

"You can't," Robert assured him. "Sap is watery and resin's like glue. And though I've never tasted resin, I assume it isn't sweet."

Dan gave a little nod to communicate that he understood. Robert tucked the bark into his backpack, and removed a re-sealable plastic bag. As Dan watched curiously, Robert reached up to one of the lower branches, and began plucking the needles. When the bag was about half full, he zipped it and returned it to his pack.

"Let's go make some tea!" he exclaimed.

Dan wasn't sure what he meant, but assumed he'd find out soon enough. The trio made their way to a clearing, led by Robert. He asked his partners to gather up a small amount of dry wood and grasses, while he himself searched for large stones. Having made an enclosed ring with the rocks, he waited for his mates to bring their materials. After placing the grass and branches in the circle, he retrieved a small magnifying glass from his pack. With the intensity of the mid-day sun, it didn't take long for the lens to ignite the dry grass beneath the branches.

"You're nothing but an overgrown boy-scout, Rob!" Chad ribbed him. Robert just smiled as he dug out the bag of pine needles, a tin cup, a small pot, and a water bottle.

"Pull out your cups, boys!" he instructed the other two.

It was the first time that Dan had opened his backpack, and he now realized why it was so heavy. Inside were all sorts of things: a first aid kit, a flashlight and water purification tablets, to name just a few items.

Robert pulled out a plastic bottle of honey, and squeezed a few spurts into the three cups.

"So how did you become such an expert on survival?" Dan asked him.

"You learn a lot about survival in the marines," Robert divulged.

"Wow! You were in the marines?"

"Yes, and I was an instructor when I retired," he added.

Dan was impressed and a bit surprised at the same time.

"You look too young to be retired," he pointed out.

"When your body's been through what mine has, retirement can't come soon enough," Robert asserted.

After removing the pot from the flame, he set it down on a level spot of ground. He then added the pine needles to steep. Dan awaited the outcome of this strange brew as he continued to delve into Robert's personal history.

"How did Chief Q manage to snag someone like you?" he wondered.

"Actually, I snagged him," Robert boasted, piquing Dan's curiosity.

"What do you mean?"

"After I retired from the marines, I became a park ranger, and I was assigned here to the Gila Forest. One day, as I was patrolling the outskirts of the park, I came across some unusual activity. It was right on the border between the park and a private acreage. That land was owned by Ronald Katzman..."

"...The billionaire?" Dan interrupted excitedly.

"That's the one."

"I look forward to meeting him," Dan announced.

"I hope you don't meet him for many, many years," Robert countered oddly.

"Why is that?"

"He passed away just a couple of months ago," Robert divulged.

"Oh. That's so sad. He didn't get to see Eos up and running," Dan lamented.

"He wasn't even that old either, and he seemed to be in good health, the last time I saw him. Anyway, in his will he left most of his money to various charities, apparently, the bulk of it to Eos. He made sure that we'll be well provided for in the future. In that regard, he put Chief Q in charge of future financial matters," noted Robert.

"Getting back to our story; although these guys were burrowing into private land, they were obviously headed in the direction of the park. So, I went over to these workers and asked what they were up to. They politely said they couldn't tell me, which is not the answer I was looking for. I asked them if they had a permit for whatever it was they were doing. That's when I could see the panic in their eyes. They told me to wait while they fetched their boss. After a few minutes, this quirky looking Native guy comes over..."

"...Chief Q?" Dan interjected again.

"In the flesh. To make a very long story short. He fessed up about the whole thing. He then offered me a place in Eos if I wouldn't rat him out. Since I know this area better than most, and I already live here, it seemed like a perfect fit. Of course, if I didn't believe in what they were trying to do, I never would have agreed. And as Chief Q pointed out, I would be able to keep an eye on them the whole time. If at any point, I thought something fishy was going on, I could always call in the authorities and shut 'em down."

"That's fascinating," Dan remarked, as Robert poured pine needle tea into their cups.

Dan took a whiff as he blew on it.

"It smells decent," he conceded.

"The important thing is that it's high in vitamin C, which will prevent scurvy," Chad preached.

"Cheers to that!" Robert proclaimed, lifting up his cup in front of his colleagues.

Their cups made a metallic clinking sound as they met.

"Cheers!" they echoed.

***

Just after sundown, there was a strong rap on the front door. Helen approached it anxiously, and took a look through the viewer. It was an ordinary looking younger man.

"Who is it?" she asked clearly.

"Public Utilities Ma'am. I'm here to turn the power back on, but I need to check your switchbox first."

"Why aren't you wearing a uniform?" she rightfully wondered.

"They called me in for overtime just after I washed it. It's still airdrying in my yard."

"Could I see some identification please?" Helen requested.

There was a short silence from the visitor, then a somewhat aggressive response.

"Do you want your power back on or not?"

"No thank you. I think I'm fine for now," she decided wisely.

Her decision did not go over well with the stranger.

"Open the damn door, you stupid hag!"

Helen's heart began to pound uncontrollably as she descended into panic mode. The unwanted visitor began to throw his body against her door. She raced to the storage closet and unlocked it with the key she had grabbed off the mantel. Pulling out a rifle, she cocked it as she scurried over to the living-room window and snatched the curtains open. Her visitor noticed her, and froze. The look in his eyes instantly transitioned from anger to fear.

Even under these circumstances, Helen still managed to keep her civility as she warned the aggressor.

"I think you better leave now before someone gets hurt!" She yelled nervously.

That was all the warning the trespasser needed. He ran off down the driveway at Olympic qualifying pace, and never looked back. Helen continued to watch the sprinting figure as it melted into the darkness. Still clutching her husband's rifle for dear life, she slowly walked away from the window. Her heart rate began to decrease, as she wiped away the dripping sweat from her forehead.

"Thank God I finally gave in to you and learned how to use this thing," she said as she gazed over at William's photo.

She could have sworn she saw the smile on his face widen, just a little.

Chapter Seven

A Voice in the Wilderness

More than a week had now passed since the power outages began, and most of the chosen ones had now settled in at Eos. On a warm and breezy early afternoon, a black Hummer pulled up at the main entrance. The gate slid open and the imposing vehicle drove straight into the multi-car garage. As soon as the driver entered the foyer of the home he was greeted, by Chad and Robert.

"Welcome back Bill!" Chad boomed. "Nice to see you again!"

"Likewise," answered Bill, as he shared firm handshakes with the other two.

"So, what's it like out there?" Robert inquired.

"Well...the first couple of days were pretty quiet. Then, about two days ago, everything took a quick turn for the worse. Now there's widespread looting of businesses, and it's starting to spread to residential areas. People are running low on supplies, and they're starting to realize this could last a while. Grocery chain warehouses are under heavy guard, but it's just a matter of time before desperation kicks in, and those come under attack by armed mobs," Bill predicted frankly.

"I don't understand why people can't just pool their resources, and help each other out," Robert said with a shake of his head.

"That's how it was at first, actually" Bill pointed out. "Then the bad apples decided to take advantage. Now the goodhearted people are afraid, and they're starting to barricade themselves. Some are migrating to areas that still have power. Personally, I don't think that's a good idea."

"Why is that?" Chad wondered.

"Well, most of the food comes from outside those areas," Bill elaborated. "As the supply starts to dwindle, and the population increases..."

"...It's a recipe for disaster," Robert concluded.

"Exactly," Bill agreed.

"How's the gasoline situation?" Chad queried.

"It varies. Some stations are using hand-pumps, and some are using spark-free generators. But the demand is much greater than the small amounts still being trucked in. Some gas stations have already closed down," Bill informed them.

"I'm glad we have our own fuel tanks here at Eos," Robert consoled them. "Any news about how other countries were affected?"

"Yeah, the solar storm affected the entire planet, but no one has it as bad as us. That EMP attack afterwards was a knockout blow. Ironically, it's the third world countries that are best equipped to deal with all this. They're not as reliant on the power grid as we are," figured Bill.

"So, it seems that we're going to be camping out here for a while," Chad concluded.

"I'm afraid so," Bill concurred. "In about ten days I'm going to return and do another assessment."

"I think Chad should go with you next time," counselled Robert, "it sounds like it's getting dangerous out there."

"Isn't that going to leave you a little shorthanded around here?" Bill worried.

"No, it's pretty calm around here so far. Plus, we have a new young recruit by the name of Dan. He's a quick learner. We already showed him how to make his own weapons and everything," Robert gushed.

Meanwhile, Chad tried to hide his disapproval of Robert's plan, and just kept quiet. He didn't like the idea of leaving Eos. Whatever his reason, he wasn't letting on about it.

***

"Good afternoon Miss Donegal!"

With tray in hand, Eve turned around to see who the familiar voice belonged to. It was Michael, who was just finishing his lunch.

"Oh hi!" I was wondering when you were going to show up!" she exclaimed.

"I just got here at daybreak. My gathering duties are finally over."

"Yeah, I've noticed a lot of new faces around here lately. Are all the chosen ones here now?"

"Pretty much. There are just two more fellas still to come. They should be here any day now."

"Thank goodness," Eve proclaimed with a sigh. "I don't mean to complain, but I don't think I could handle any more mouths to feed. I don't know how Chef Steven keeps that smile on his face all the time. I only put in three two-hour shifts at meal times, with the occasional menu planning. He practically lives in the kitchen."

"That's why he's our chosen chef. Trust me, there's nowhere else he'd rather be." Michael assured her. "Having said that, if he ever gets burned out, just let me know. I make a mean peanut butter and jelly sandwich."

"I'm sure our fourteen residents with peanut allergies will take great comfort in that."

"You can't please 'em all," Michael shrugged mischievously.

"Well, I have to get back to work," Eve said with a smile. "I'll see you around the cave sometime."

"Oh, for sure. Just look for the best dressed dude in town," Michael bragged, as he flipped his tie out of his vest.

By the time Dan had walked into the cafeteria, most of the diners had already cleared out, including Michael. He slowly swung open the kitchen doors and poked his head in. Chef Steven and Eve were busy putting away food and utensils, as two other couples washed the dishes.

"Hi guys! Sorry I'm late. Any chance at some leftovers?"

"Hey! Looks like Robin Hood and G.I. Jane had a son together!" teased the chef, who hadn't seen Dan in his new guardian outfit yet.

"Wow! You look awesome!" Eve gushed.

Dan entered in fully, and removed the quiver of arrows from his back.

"Check this out," he said as he turned around.

"Is that the latest fashion out here, the sci-fi look?" Eve asked him.

"It's a solar vest," Dan explained. "That's a flexible solar panel. It charges the batteries in this pocket here." He pointed to the small pocket in his upper left sleeve. "Our engineer just put the finishing touches on it. They also gave me this cool watch with a zillion functions; a walkie-talkie, super powerful flashlight…"

"…No gun?" Eve interrupted.

"No. I don't have a permit," Dan informed her. "Anyway, all these gadgets run on these small batteries that charge in this vest. It's the coolest thing ever."

"How does the vest work if it's covered up?"

"It isn't completely covered actually, but it's when we've stopped to rest that it does most of its charging. Which is quite often for me. This equipment weighs a tonne," Dan whined.

"Well, I'm so glad you're getting down with your new line of work, Mr. Barista. So how does a nice big chicken Caesar salad sound?"

"Sounds wonderful. Especially the part about 'big'. I'm *starving*," Dan announced, "and I need the energy. I'm about to go out on my first solo patrol."

"Really? That sounds a bit dangerous," worried Eve.

"No, it's basically just going for a walk around the property. I've done it with Chad and Robert a few times. Only twice did we come upon anybody, a couple of campers."

"Weren't they wondering who you guys were?" Eve asked.

"Yeah, and we told them the truth. We told them we were private security for some nearby residents. They just assumed we were only talking about the estate."

Chef Steven walked over holding a large bowl of Caesar salad.

"Here you go my friend! Is this big enough?"

"Oh, that should definitely do, thank you so much," said the grateful guardian.

As he planted himself at a nearby table, everyone got back to their tasks. Dan didn't know if it was because he was so hungry, but the salad was the best he could ever remember eating. Then again, every meal Chef Steven had prepared so far had been brilliant.

***

As he made his way off the estate path, Dan couldn't help but wonder what life was like back home now. Here amid the serenity of nature, with the birds singing and the trees subtly dancing in the warm breeze, everything seemed so normal.

Winding his way underneath the pines, he surveyed the ground ahead. Normally, as with most people, he would pretty much look straight ahead until he stepped in something unpleasant. However, with his recent training, he was now in the habit of reading his surroundings. Which is probably why he noticed an odd-shaped object just a few feet ahead. As he bent down to grab it, he immediately recognized it as a spearhead. It was very similar to the one Robert had help him fashion from a sharp rock, just a few days earlier. He removed the combined backpack and quiver from his back. He now had two spearheads in his arsenal. As he zipped up the bag, he fleetingly wondered who might have lost it. He didn't have to wonder very long at all.

"That belongs to *me*!" thundered a voice from behind him.

Dan nearly lost his balance and fell over, as he quickly stood and turned. He couldn't believe what he was seeing, as his heart threatened to beat right out of his chest. He found himself face to face with a caveman, of all things. The man had long, messy brown hair and a beard. He was dressed in some type of animal fur, and held a spear that was pointed towards Dan in a most threatening fashion. In the back of his mind, Dan hoped he had stumbled onto a movie set. Unfortunately, the lack of any cameramen nearby made it highly unlikely.

"Are you one of Herod's men?" the caveman demanded to know.

"W...what? Who's Harold?" stammered Dan.

"Not Harold! Herod! Don't play games with me!"

"I'm not playing games with you sir. I don't know who you're talking about," he professed honestly.

"Then who are you? Why are you dressed like them?"

"My name is Daniel."

"Daniel?" he echoed, in a calmer voice.

"Yes sir," Dan replied politely.

"I've heard of you. You're one of the chosen ones," the wild man stated. Dan was completely shocked.

"How do you know about the chosen ones?" he asked with confused amazement.

"I often read the scriptures. I know everything," the stranger boasted.

Dan couldn't say the same. But he did remember one of the stories a foster parent had read him once. It was a Bible story about Daniel and the lion's den. It suddenly became quite clear to Dan, that this man wasn't living in the same reality as him. He also noticed that he no longer had that murderous look in his eye. His heart slowed a few paces as he tried to talk his way out of the mess.

"And what is your name sir?"

"My name is John. You may call me Johnny."

"It's very nice to meet you Johnny," Dan said in a rather unconvincing tone. "Where did you come from?"

"I came from the city."

"Me too," Dan said in a soothing tone. "I'm from Albuquerque. Which city are you from?"

"El Paso," Johnny replied simply, as he lowered the spear.

"So, what are you doing all the way out here?" the now much more relaxed Dan couldn't help but ask.

"I fled the city to escape its destruction on the day of judgement," Johnny started to rant. "I am the voice of one crying out in the wilderness! Repent, for the kingdom of God is at hand!"

Dan suddenly recognized some of Johnny's words from those childhood Bible lessons. If he wasn't mistaken, they were the words of John the Baptist.

"Let me guess. You like to eat locusts and honey. Am I right?" Dan asked enthusiastically.

"What are you, nuts?"

"Well, I just thought since they're so nutritious and all..." Dan patronized.

"Who in their right mind would eat bugs? I like fish, berries, and roasted birds mostly," Johnny educated him.

"So, you live close by here then?" Dan asked.

"Yes," Johnny affirmed, as he pointed to the east. "I live in a cliff dwelling about a mile from here."

"So, what brings you around this specific area? Are you looking for food?"

"No, I've been watching Herod and his men come and go from the palace."

Suddenly, Johnny lifted his spear and pointed it at Dan again.

"You still haven't told me why you're dressed like them!"

Dan started to think quickly, not wanting to lose the ground he seemed to have just gained.

"I'm not really one of his men. I infiltrated his home a couple of weeks ago. I'm *also* keeping an eye on him," he bluffed.

"So, you're a spy then?" Johnny asked, as he apparently took the bait.

"Yes!" Dan declared happily.

"You better be awfully careful young Daniel. If Herod discovers you're a spy, he'll kill you without so much as blinking. He's an evil snake!"

"Yes, I know. Just have faith in God, he'll protect us."

Dan felt bad about using the man's beliefs against him, but he couldn't think of any other way to console him. He then remembered the object that had seemingly gotten him into this tight spot. He reached into his backpack, which he was clutching at his side, and pulled out the spearhead.

"Here, I almost forgot. This is yours," Dan offered with an open hand.

"No. Please keep it. I would be honored if you kept it as a remembrance of me," Johnny implored.

With a warm smile, Dan returned it to the bag.

"Thank you very much Johnny. It was a pleasure to meet you, but I really should get back to the palace now, before they become suspicious."

"May God go with you, Daniel."

"And with you also," Dan stated as he walked by Johnny, heading back in the direction of Eos.

Johnny patted him on the shoulder. Dan responded with a slow wave of his right hand and a smile.

When he arrived back at the security room, Dan found Chad and another guardian talking over an open map. They were both leaning on the table, and had turned their heads when they heard the door opening.

"Hi guys!" Dan greeted them enthusiastically.

"Hey Danny boy! What's new and exciting?" Chad responded, as his companion smiled.

"Funny you should ask!" Dan said with amusement. "I came across this stranger just outside the property."

"Another camper?" Chad guessed.

"You *could* say that. But he was more like a hermit. The thing is, he thinks he's John the Baptist, if I'm not mistaken."

"Sounds harmless enough," Chad opined.

"Well, I think *I'll* be fine with him. He thinks I'm the Daniel of the Bible, so I went along with it. I told him I was spying on Herod and his men, which would be you guys. I'm afraid anyone else in a guardian's uniform might be at risk. He pointed a spear at me a couple of times before we became friends."

"Thanks for the heads up. If we come across him, we'll try and reason with him. If that doesn't work, we should be able to scare him off with a gunshot into the air," Chad concluded.

"We should make sure everyone else is aware of him," Dan counseled. I don't want him to get hurt, though. He's obviously ill."

"I'll take care of it, Chad assured him. Don't worry, this is a minor problem compared to what's going on in the outside world. Which reminds me. Bill is back. When you see him, ask him to debrief you on his outing."

"Will do," said Dan.

"Listen. Why don't you call it a shift? Sounds like you've had enough excitement for one day," suggested Robert.

"Great. I'll see you guys tomorrow then."

With dinner still a few hours away, Dan figured a stroll in the gardens might do him some good. Then, he'd check out the river at the far end of the caverns, which he hadn't seen yet. As he walked amid the hydrangeas and rhododendrons, the wheels in his mind began to slow, from their dizzying pace. He had been so preoccupied lately with his new home, job, and friends, that he rarely had time to think about his pre-Eos existence.

He reached into his oversized pants pocket and pulled out his old friend, the envelope. It was a little worse for wear, but it remained sealed. He held it at his right-hand side as he walked along, staring up at the shafts of afternoon light, and contemplating his life. As the days had passed, he had made new friends and discovered a new sense of purpose. Even more importantly, he was gradually developing a relationship with Eve. On the other hand, this envelope represented confusion, anxiety, and doubt.

By the time he reached the river, he had also arrived at a decision. As far as he was concerned, the events of two weeks ago, were like a reset switch being flipped. He had been given a clean slate, and he liked the new story that was being written. His conclusion; it was time to let go of the past.

Dan stopped in front of the streaming turquoise waters. The rumbling of the river was like a voice, asking something of him. He responded by tossing the envelope into its cool embrace. His offering was not accepted however, as the letter was quickly deposited onto a nearby embankment.

Dan was unaware of its fate though, as he had already turned and walked away. The unwanted envelope had barely come to a standstill, when a hand reached down and lifted it from the sandy ground. The one handling it looked at the address. It had come from the offices of a private investigator.

Chapter Eight

A Priest and a Rabbi Walk into a Cave...

With the bright, late September sunshine warming her back, Helen eased herself into the backyard picnic-table and carefully set down the rifle. She had been feeling like a prisoner in her own home. This retreat into the yard is exactly what she needed. The night before, she had heard someone tampering with the back window. Luckily, she was still awake, and was able to scare them off by making a big noise in the kitchen. What if she had been asleep and hadn't heard it? she thought to herself. She missed Mr. Personality, her Golden Retriever, even more now. She wished she had gotten around to replacing him after he had passed away last spring. But at the time, she felt he was irreplaceable.

Helen had barely finished spreading some bird seed out, before a small flock of birds came swooping down on the table. Up until a few weeks ago, this had been a daily ritual for her. The birds probably knew what was coming as soon as she sat down.

"Oh, I'm sorry, did you little dears miss me?" She asked them.

One of the sparrows tilted its head up toward her as if he understood, then went quickly back to its feast. Their innocence and fragility were an ironic contrast to the shotgun laying beside them, with its violent power.

***

Dan was feeling rather dejected as he exited the security room. Bill had just updated him on the living conditions back in Santa Fe, and Dan assumed it would be no different in Albuquerque. Food shortages, nightly curfews, no running water; some of these things he hadn't really considered when he thought about a power outage.

Dan was headed toward the second cavern, where the gardens are, to do a routine patrol. It had more to do with checking the birdfeeders and the condition of the trees, than with any real security concerns. The gardeners had their hands full with helping the farmer tend to the crops, which was obviously a priority. As he made his way onto the main path which connects the caves, he noticed Robert and a couple of older gentlemen coming toward him. They were both dressed in black. One was wearing a suit and tie. The other seemed to be dressed in priestly garb. Everyone smiled, as they all came together.

"Dan, I'd like you to meet Father James and Rabbi Yosef. They're our two final residents, both hailing from Chicago," said Robert.

Nice to meet you, Sirs," Dan said, as they exchanged handshakes.

"The pleasure is all ours," responded Rabbi Yosef, for the both of them.

"By the way, is there a bar in this facility?" inquired Father James.

"A bar?" Dan asked.

"Yes, so the rabbi and myself can walk into it," joked the priest.

Everyone chuckled immediately, except Dan, who needed a few seconds to process.

"Oh, I get it. I wish I had thought of that," he regretted with a smile.

"I thought about that right away," claimed Robert. "But then I thought to myself - nah, it's too easy. Anyway, if you're not too busy Dan, could you escort our newest cellmates to their quarters?"

"Certainly. Where exactly would that be?" Dan asked.

Robert took his manual out of his right pants pocket, and snuck a quick peek.

"There are a few vacant suites at the far north end, just after the family area," Robert indicated.

"No problem. Please follow me gentlemen," Dan requested.

Robert went to tend to other business as Dan led the pair along the path.

"So, is it just a coincidence that you're both from Chicago, and that you both arrived here at the same time?" Dan wondered.

"Oh no," Father James assured him. "We're childhood friends. We grew up together on the same street. I recommended Rabbi Yosef to my mentor, when they mentioned they were looking for a rabbi."

"So, was Michael your mentor as well?" the rabbi asked Dan.

"Actually, I didn't have a mentor. Chief Q allowed me in with a young lady named Eve. *She* was the chosen one."

"Wow! So, you were handpicked by Chief Q himself. You must be a very special individual," insinuated Father James.

"That's the strange thing. I don't have any special skills, and I'm not a religious person either. Until quite recently, I thought that Joan of Arc was Noah's wife."

The two clerics shared a quick laugh.

"That's a good one. Can I use that?" asked the priest.

"Sure, be my guest," Dan offered.

"Well," the rabbi chimed in, "I've heard that Chief Q is a very wise man, so you must have *some* redeeming qualities."

"I hope you're right Sir," Dan said hopefully. "Just out of curiosity, how did you leave Chicago without telling your superiors?"

"First of all, we're both retired. As for Rabbi, he doesn't really have superiors. He's kind of his own boss. As for myself, I had to tell my Bishop without compromising Eos. So, during confession, I informed him that I was coming here, without offering too many details. Under the seal of the confessional, he can never speak of it to anyone. It was kind of sly, but hey, I'm Irish. It's in my blood," Father chuckled.

"And you both didn't leave any family behind?" Dan inquired.

"Father James never married of course, and my wife passed away from cancer many years ago," stated Rabbi Yosef. "We didn't have any children unfortunately, and I never remarried."

"I'm really sorry to hear about your wife," Dan lamented genuinely.

"Thank you," replied the rabbi.

"How about siblings and relatives?" Dan pressed curiously.

"Oh, I have family scattered throughout the country," Said Father James. And I believe Rabbi Yosef does as well. But we consider all of mankind to be our family."

"I'm almost afraid to ask," Dan continued, "but how was the situation in Chicago when you two left?"

There was silence for a few moments, which in itself spoke volumes to Dan.

"I won't sugar-coat it for you son," said the priest. "People are quickly turning into barbarians. I'm afraid people today are just too selfish and impatient, to deal with any hardships."

Upon hearing this, Dan's face revealed his concern. The other two looked at each other. It was evident that they knew one another very well, for they could communicate with each other through their eyes. Father James spoke for the two of them, as they approached their dwellings.

"Listen young man. If you ever have anything you need to talk about, we're both available, anytime."

"Thanks. I'll probably take you up on that sometime."

When Dan had dismissed himself, the two men stood in front of their suites and chatted.

"I sense that Dan is troubled by something, more so than just the obvious current events," Father James opined.

"Me too. But I also feel that he has very good intentions," added Rabbi Yosef.

"I totally agree," Father James concurred. "Well, we're back to where we started. We're next door neighbors again."

"Yes, it's amazing how life plays itself out, isn't it?"

***

The sticker on the door warned of alarms on the premises. That was irrelevant to the hooded figure knocking on it. Having received no response, he sprayed some sort of substance into the keyhole, before inserting the stolen locksmith's tool into it. Within three seconds, he was opening the door, allowing muted sunlight to flood the dark hallway.

Once inside, he began to ransack the apartment quickly, lest the occupants soon returned. His large gym-bag contained only the entry tool, small spray can, and a flashlight. There was plenty of room left over for small valuables or cash.

Having flung open most of the drawers in the suite, he could tell that the occupant had probably vacated. Jewellery boxes were empty, and he could find no important documents, such as passports or certificates.

In the bedroom, on top of the antique wooden nightstand, sat a fair-sized jade sculpture. Beside it, was a portrait of an older, sophisticated looking couple, with an attractive young lady sitting in front of them. What the burglar judged to be an eagle, was in fact a Phoenix, rising up from a green, molten mound. As a consolation prize, it would suffice. His bag was still very empty, but much heavier, after placing the semi-precious piece inside it.

Upon re-entering the living room, the large aquarium caught his eye. It was completely silent, and very dark, but he could still make out some moving shapes inside. Seeing a small, plastic container of fish food on a nearby shelf, he grabbed it and opened the tank's lid. Rubbing a few pinches of the flakes over the water, he watched the famished fish come to the surface and feast. He then closed the lid, placed the container beside the tank, and grabbed his gym-bag.

On his way to the front door, he glimpsed a tiny box near the baseboard. Picking it up, he could see it was a jewellery box, with a fancy letter 'D' on the cover. With only the light from the living room window, he couldn't make out the small words under the logo; Donegan jewellers. He *was, h*owever, able to see the ring he found inside, and the large gem mounted onto it.

In her haste, the occupant had dropped it on the way out. One person's misfortune is another one's gain.

"This is turning out to be a pretty good day after all," he uttered in an almost inaudible whisper.

If the fish could talk, they would probably have said the same thing.

Chapter Nine

Return to Sender

Dark, menacing clouds were starting to roll in; pregnant with the promise of rain. Maybe they were on their way down to the desert, where they were most needed. If they did decide to set up shop here, in the Gila wilderness, they would still be appreciated. It hadn't rained in a few weeks.

Dan remembered seeing a poncho in his backpack, so he wasn't too concerned about any potential storm.

"Johnny!" he called out at the top of his lungs. "Hello!"

After Dan called out a few more times, the unkempt hermit casually walked into his field of view, from the direction of the cliffs. He appeared so stoic and mysterious, that Dan became even more unsettled than he had already been.

"Hi Johnny. Do you remember me?" Dan asked hopefully.

"Of course, Brother Daniel! How goes the battle against the forces of evil?" he thundered.

"Um...I think we're winning," Dan proposed meekly.

"Good to hear!" Johnny responded, as he approached Dan. "Just don't turn your back on that golden-haired snake!"

Dan assumed that he was referring to Chad.

"You certainly don't mince your words," Dan conceded. "By the way, what did you do for a living back in El Paso? If you don't mind me asking."

"I was the sales manager for an ad agency," answered Johnny, who was now right in front of him.

"Oh, that's interesting," Dan alleged, trying to hide his surprise.

He found it odd that someone with such a normal job, could end up falling through the cracks.

"Did you enjoy your work?"

"At first, it was okay. Then, I came to hate it with all my being," Johnny replied bluntly.

"I'm sorry to hear that. I wish I could give you helpful advice for your situation, but I'm afraid I'm not qualified. However, I *can* offer you this," Dan said, as he unzipped his backpack.

He pulled out a plastic bowl and popped the lid off. Inside, was a generous portion of Chef Steven's now famous chicken Caesar salad.

"My friends inside the palace made this."

"Are you sure they are trustworthy? What if they poisoned it?" Johnny cautioned.

"Oh, don't worry. They're on our side. Plus, I had some of it last night, and I feel fine," Dan assured him.

Before Dan could pull out a plastic fork, Johnny grabbed some salad with his grimy, gnarled fingers. He must have found it as delicious as everyone before him, because he barely took any breaths between handfuls. After polishing off the entire bowl, he returned it to Dan and wiped his mouth with the back of his hand.

"You're a good man, Daniel," Johnny declared.

As they say, the quickest way to a man's heart, is via the stomach.

***

Eve pulled the needle and white thread from the jacket one last time. She then held up Chef Steven's uniform to admire her handiwork. Somehow, he had managed to snag it on a shelf corner inside the walk-in cooler.

She hung the white jacket on a chair and put away her sewing accessories. Suddenly, there was a rap on the door. Perfect timing, she thought to herself. She was right by the door and opened it immediately.

"Oh hi! You finally took me up on my offer to see the place," she declared.

"I happened to be in the neighborhood, so I thought I'd drop by," Dan claimed. "Did that just sound as cliché to you as it did to me?" he added.

"Very much so, but you're forgiven. Come on in," Eve offered eagerly.

As he entered the smallish suite, Dan looked around.

"You obviously have some serious decorating skills. How did you manage to make it look so upscale? My suite was exactly the same as yours, and now, it looks like my old apartment," Dan admitted.

"Old habits are hard to break I guess. For the both of us. So, listen, I don't have a coffee maker here, but how about a nice herbal tea?" Eve offered.

"Sounds wonderful," he said, as he took the seat in front of him.

After filling the kettle and turning it on, Eve took the other seat across the table from Dan.

"So, I'm assuming you're just fulfilling your duties as guardian, and checking up on me?"

"Actually, I was wondering if I could talk to you about something," Dan asked rather seriously.

"Of course," she declared.

"There's something I've been keeping to myself, and it's really starting to bother me," Dan said.

"What is it?" Eve asked with concern.

"You see...I was adopted," Dan said ashamedly, his eyes aiming down at his interlaced hands.

"So, when you said your parents had moved away, you meant your adoptive parents?"

"No. That didn't work out actually. I ended up in foster care. Altogether, I've had three sets of parents, not including my natural ones.

And I have no idea where any of them are now. I don't blame them, though. Those immature friends I was telling you about, and myself, would be at fault there I'm afraid. When I said that they had moved away, I was just making that up," Dan clarified. "Technically, I was lying, and I'm very sorry for that. I had just met you, and I couldn't bring myself to be that open with you yet."

"I understand," Eve responded compassionately, "but you obviously feel differently now."

"Yes. And you're one of the few people I've ever told. Since I was a kid I've always hidden that from whoever I could."

"Why?" It's nothing to be ashamed of. It isn't anything you did, or had control over," she reasoned.

Without saying it, Dan seemed to accept her observation.

"Anyway, just days before I met you, I obtained the names and location of my birth parents."

Eve waited for details, but they weren't coming. Dan really seemed to be having difficulty even speaking.

"And?" she asked anxiously.

"That's the problem. I never opened the envelope. I was waiting for a moment of courage, and then all this happened. So, I put it off until I would feel more settled in. But then, I got really comfortable with all of you."

Even though he had just tried not to single out Eve, his eyes couldn't hide the fact that he was talking about *her* in particular.

"I decided I was finally going to stop torturing myself about the past, and start off fresh. So, I never opened it. In fact, I destroyed it. Then I heard from Bill that things were really deteriorating in the cities. Yesterday, the two final chosen ones arrived, and they said it's basically anarchy out there. Now I wish I hadn't been so hasty in my decision."

"Why is that?" asked Eve.

"I mean, I don't know my parents at all, but they're still my family. I don't feel right, not knowing if they need help or not. It's hard to travel around now, and even if I did go back to Albuquerque, I can't be sure I'd be able to contact the P.I."

"You mean Stevenson Investigations?" Eve asked casually, completely stunning Dan.

"How could you possibly know that? You must have seen me holding the letter at some point," he assumed.

"Actually, I noticed you grab it just before we left your apartment, and I saw you fumbling with it on the way here. But that isn't how I know the name," she declared.

Dan's eyebrows shrunk together in confusion.

"Remember the other day when you were down by the river?"

"Yes," Dan replied curtly, wondering how she knew that.

"I saw you before you left the gardens. I called out to you, but you didn't hear me. So instead of yelling and disturbing the peace, I decided to catch up with you. As I approached you, you threw the letter in the river and walked away. You didn't notice that it only made it about ten feet. I saw it wash up on the bank and picked it up. I was careful not to damage it. I carried it by the corner until I got back here."

"So, you still have it then!" Dan exclaimed enthusiastically.

"Yeah. I figured it was very personal, so I was waiting to catch you alone."

Eve got up and went to retrieve the letter from her drawer. She sat back down as she carefully handed it to Dan.

"You don't know how many times I felt like opening it," she confessed.

"Boy, I know *that* feeling," he told her.

"I have to be honest. I was afraid you might be hiding a dark secret or something," Eve admitted.

"That's a possibility. I mean, my parents could be notorious criminals or something, for all I know. That's one of the reasons I never opened it," he elaborated. "I wonder if it's still readable," Dan wondered as he scanned it nervously.

"I'm assuming it's printed, not written in pen," she said. "So, it should be readable. It seems a bit water-stained, but it's completely dry now."

"Well, this is the moment of truth I guess," Dan said as he began to tear open the flap.

Suddenly, the water kettle started whistling, and he stopped.

"Oh. Water's ready," Eve announced, as she quickly stood up and briskly made her way to the kettle. "That's okay! Don't wait for me. Just open it while I make the tea."

Dan forcefully ripped open the rest of the flap. He gingerly removed the somewhat stiff letter from it's envelope. As he unfolded the two-page letter, he could see it was still legible, despite the yellowish water stains.

"Can you make it out?" Eve asked, as she poured the steaming water into a modest teapot.

Dan didn't seem to hear her as he scanned the papers hypnotically. Eve figured it best not to distract him, as she patiently awaited any details. While waiting for the tea to steep, she brought two white mugs over to the table. Finally, he lowered the letter and looked blankly at Eve.

"What is it?" she asked timidly.

"My father already passed away," Dan said rather robotically.

"Oh, I'm so sorry. How about your mother?" she asked cautiously.

"She lives in Phoenix. It says here she's widowed with no other children, and hasn't remarried."

"So, your mother is the only immediate family you have then," said Eve. "How long has your father been deceased?"

"This says he died during military service in Iraq. And it happened just months before I was born."

"That's so sad," Eve mourned. "That might explain why you were given up for adoption, though" she pointed out.

"That's exactly what I was thinking," Dan said, as he blew on his hot tea.

By now, the aroma of flower petals and berries had infused the atmosphere.

"Hopefully, everything will be back to normal soon. Then you can try to contact her."

"No," Dan said in a low tone. "It could be too late by then. I have to find her now."

"What do you mean?" asked a dumbfounded Eve.

"I have to get to Phoenix as soon as I can. She may be alone for all I know. I couldn't live with myself, not knowing if she needs help or not."

"But it sounds like it could be dangerous out there," worried Eve.

"That's *exactly* why I have to try and find her," Dan reasoned. "I'm going to tell Robert first thing in the morning, and I guess I should speak to Chief Q as well."

"How would you get there," Eve asked as she held her mug with both hands.

"Hopefully, I can find someone who will lend me their car."

"Well, you're more than welcome to use mine...but...do you really think this is a good idea?" Eve stuttered.

"I really don't feel like I have any other option," Dan stated plainly.

He could see Eve was rather unsettled by this turn of events.

Dan took a long sip of his tea, in an attempt to break their gaze. But when he lowered the cup, Eve was still looking directly at him.

"So, I guess this would be goodbye then?" she asked sadly.

"Just for a while. If I find her, and she's safe, I'll come right back here. If she needs me, then I'll either stay with her for a while, or take her back to Albuquerque. No matter what happens, I'll find you again as soon as I can. It won't be long before you see me walking into your jewellery store again," he said in a consoling tone.

Eve gave him a brave grin, but it didn't look very convincing. Having finished about half his drink, Dan stood up.

"I better go look for Chief Q and start preparing for my trip to Phoenix. I can't thank you enough for saving that letter for me, as well as everything else you've done."

Eve put down her tea and arose from the table.

"You're more than welcome. And thanks for confiding in me. If you ever have any problems, I'm here for you," Eve said with visible sincerity.

Dan felt that he should give her a hug at this point, but for some reason, he couldn't work up the courage. Instead, he gave himself an out.

"I'll make sure I see you again before I go," he said uncomfortably.

"You better. Otherwise I won't give you my car-keys," she half-joked. She then walked him to the door, and the two said good night to each other, as if it were for the last time.

After closing the door behind her, Eve took a big breath and gave out a sad sigh, as she fought back the tears forming in her eyes.

***

With a heavy heart, Dan knocked on Chief Q's door. It opened almost immediately.

"Good evening young man! entre vous," the leader of Eos greeted him, as he swung the door wide open.

This was the first time Dan had been here, and he was surprised to see it was the same size as all the other single units. The only difference was the décor, which unsurprisingly, was mostly Native American. Just as Eve had done earlier, the Chief offered his guest some tea, which Dan politely accepted. Dan explained the situation to his makeshift mentor, who listened with great interest and compassion. Surprisingly, he even offered to accept Dan's mother into the facilities, if he could find her, and she were in need.

"You mean you'd be willing to accept a total stranger into Eos unseen?" Dan asked with a little surprise.

"I have confidence in your judgement. If you'd feel comfortable bringing her here, then I'd feel comfortable in accepting her," Chief Q claimed.

"I can't tell you how much I appreciate your understanding and hospitality," Dan gushed.

"There's only one condition," Chief Q added. "I can't let you go alone. Bill and Chad were supposed to leave for Santa Fe in a couple of days anyway. We'll change the destination to Phoenix, and you can leave first thing in the morning."

"You have no idea how happy you've made me Sir," Dan stated with gratitude and relief.

"Hey. Here at Eos, if *you're* not happy, then *we* are," his host replied.

"Huh?" Dan grinned.

"Yes. I *was* trying to be funny," Chief Q replied with a straight face, before laughing aloud and giving Dan a hug.

Oddly enough, Dan now regretted even more not having given Eve an embrace, before leaving her suite. He suddenly realized he had hidden and unresolved issues.

He left Chief Q's place feeling so much better than he had in a long time. He now felt closer to fulfillment than he had ever felt before in his life. It was as if finding his mother was the final piece of the puzzle. However, in the back of his mind he knew there was still work to do to find her. And of course, he also felt anxious for her safety in the meantime. These past few weeks had been a real rollercoaster ride, with so many ups and downs. Hopefully things would continue to look up from here. He wanted to run back to Eve's place and share the good news with her. But it was getting late, and she might be in bed already.

As he made his way through the lit cavern back to his dwelling, he planned out the next day's itinerary. He would go have breakfast and quickly pull Eve aside and tell her the plan. Then he would talk to Robert and the other guardians at the security room morning scrum. Finally, he would say farewell to Eve, and be on his way. Since he was far too excited to sleep right away, he figured he might as well start packing when he arrived back home. Hopefully it would be a one day trip. But under the circumstances, they couldn't afford to make assumptions.

***

Eve still didn't like the idea of Dan leaving Eos, but she felt so much better about it now. At breakfast, Dan had happily explained the new situation to her. He was so glad to see her smile again, after the previous day's less than gleeful tea-party.

As he strolled from the cafeteria to his workstation, he noticed how the filtered morning light gave the caverns a beautiful postcard-like quality. The two birds chasing each other over his head, provided the finishing touch to the masterpiece.

When he entered the security room, the five other guardians were all there.

"Good morning guys," Dan greeted them.

"Good morning," they replied in relative unison.

"Sorry I'm late. I had to talk to my friend Eve," Dan said apologetically.

"That's okay. We'll just deduct it off your paycheque," Robert joked.

"You didn't happen to see Chief Q yet today, have you?" Dan wondered.

"As a matter of fact, he left just minutes ago," Robert informed him. "So, here's how it's going to work. We'll be using two vehicles; a pick-up and a Hummer, in case there's any serious mechanical issue along the way. Phoenix is a five-hour drive from here, so you'll have to leave here before sun-up, to allow you to leave *there* before nightfall. If you can't find your mother in the allotted time, you'll have to decide if you want to return here, or keep searching on your own. In which case, you'd have to find your own transportation back."

Robert paused for a moment to let his words sink in.

"Sounds fair," Dan agreed with a nod.

"Personally, I suggest you return right away if you can't find her. Because basically, it means she could be anywhere. The longer you stay in the city, the greater your risk. Not only from physical attacks, but from disease as well. You have to remember, there's no running water. The water pressure died out long ago, and the sewers are backed up. Disposal of human waste will be a major problem. This was supposed to be purely a surveillance run; obviously that plan has now changed. It'll be a little riskier, considering that you'll be entering residential areas on foot. However, both

Bill and Chad will be carrying firearms, so you should be covered at all times.

"...About that," interrupted Chad, "I was thinking if it wouldn't be better for you to take my place instead, Robert."

"Why is that," Robert asked curiously.

"Well I mean, it sounds a bit like a military operation now. You and Bill are the two with the best credentials for that. I'm just a car salesman after all."

"Seriously?" Dan interjected.

"Hey, we all gotta make a living," Chad shrugged.

"Oh no, that's not what I meant," Dan clarified. "It's just that when I first met you, I got the *impression* you were a used car salesman."

"*New* and used to be precise. But good observation nonetheless."

"That's not a bad idea, actually," Bill chimed in. Chad pretty much knows what he's doing around here now, and it *has* been very quiet. I think the extra protection it would afford Dan is a good trade off."

"Okay then, I'll tell you what," Robert acquiesced. I'll run it past the Chief. If he okays the idea, then it's a go."

"Sounds good," Chad accepted eagerly.

***

Just before sunrise on the following morning, there was a buzz of activity in the foyer of the house. The three guardians were getting ready to leave for Phoenix. The black Hummer and a grey pickup were idling in the driveway. Chief Q, Chad and Eve were all there to see them off. Even Rabbi Yosef and Father James had shown up to offer support. Chief Q had a prayer feather, which he offered to Dan. The quill was wrapped in blue and white beads and leather straps. Dan tied it to his backpack as Chief Q explained the meaning behind it. He told Dan how birds were considered the most sacred animals to the Natives, and that feathers were a gift from the Great Spirit. When one prayed with the feathers, the birds would carry those prayers up to Heaven.

"Thank you very much. It's really beautiful," Dan said. "Although I have to be honest with you. I really don't know how to pray."

"I think everyone knows how to pray, when they really need to. It just comes naturally," shared the rabbi. "When we Jews pray, we always ask that God's will be done in each situation, rather than asking for a certain outcome. That way, you always know you're praying for the right thing."

"Sometimes we just need a little reminder," added the Chief. That feather should do the trick."

"That's all very sound advice," contributed Father James. "I don't know what more I could add. Would you three mind if I just gave you a quick blessing?"

"Not at all," said Bill.

Dan and Robert also agreed. As Father James pleaded for their collective safety and peace of mind, the three bowed their heads. Afterwards, Bill made the sign of the cross.

Seconds later, Chad walked in from the driveway.

"Everything is packed and ready to go! You guys should head out now. The clock is ticking," he reminded them.

"Could I just talk with Eve for a minute?" Dan requested solemnly, as he looked her way.

"No problem son," Robert said. "We'll be waiting for you outside."

"I think we should all wait outside actually," Chief Q suggested politely.

After they'd all stepped out, Dan walked over to Eve and stood about two feet in front of her.

"You know, none of this would be possible without you. If I hadn't met you I'd probably be wandering around in Phoenix right now, wondering what my next move would be, even if I *had* found my mother. Thanks for always being in the right place at the right time."

"You started it," Eve replied with a smile. "Just make sure you don't get yourself into trouble out there. If things don't work out for you right now, you can always go back again later," she advised him.

Dan's only response was to move in closer to her. They then shared an embrace, which just seemed to come naturally. It wasn't the awkward experience Dan had been dreading either. On the contrary, he found it quite liberating. So much so, that it gave him the courage to kiss her on the forehead as well. It was a goose-bump inducing moment for both of them, but not one that they could savor very long.

"Come on Dan, time's a wasting!" Chad yelled out from the driveway.

"I think I've overstayed my welcome," Dan said as he turned toward the open door.

"Not with *me* you haven't," Eve replied as she followed him out to the driveway.

"I'll see you when I get back," Dan told her as he walked out into the cool morning air, toward the waiting vehicles.

As he waved and said goodbye to everyone, Eve called out to him with an almost angry tone.

"You *better* make sure you come back! You still owe me five dollars for that bottle of water!"

Dan grinned at her as he closed the passenger door of the Hummer. No one else knew exactly what Eve was referring to, but they all understood her intentions. Father James and the rabbi exchanged a knowing glance, as they smiled at each other.

Chapter Ten

Watch for the Curveball

When his eyes fluttered open, it took Dan a fleeting moment to remember where he was.

"Good morning princess. How was your beauty sleep?" Bill teased.

"Oh... sorry I dozed off on you like that."

"No need to apologize. People always fall asleep when I tell them my life story," Bill stated light-heartedly.

"It's not that," Dan assured his escort. "I should have gone to bed earlier last night but..."

"Eve?" Bill guessed.

"Yeah. We got to talking and the time just flew by."

"So, are you two officially an item now, or are you still 'just friends'?"

"I'm not sure. I still don't know exactly how she feels about me," Dan responded frankly.

"I do. She's crazy about you. And you feel the same way about her."

"Why do you say that?" Dan pressed curiously.

"It's as plain as the nose on your face. Or at least...the one on mine," Bill realized, as he groped his Roman nose with his left hand. "Anyhow, while you were sleeping, you missed the best sunrise ever. There were a few clouds above the horizon; and the best way I can describe it is...they looked like puffs of burning magenta, with neon orange linings."

"Your poetic skills need a little work, but I get the picture. Oh well, there'll be more sunrises," Dan said dismissively.

"I wish I shared your optimism young man, but that's not always the case."

"Yeah, you're right. I'm glad I didn't say something dumb like that to Eve."

"Oh, that's right, she was left orphaned just a few years back, wasn't she?"

"Yeah. We talked about that last night, actually. I don't think she's quite over it yet," Dan figured.

"I can imagine." Bill responded.

"That's why she understands why I have to do this." Dan stated.

"What's going on *here*?" Bill exclaimed suddenly, as he slowed to a crawl.

Robert slowly pulled over to the side of the road, with Bill and Dan following right behind.

"Whoa!" Bill yelled loudly, startling Dan in the process.

The front, right tire had come clean off the pickup and rolled into the scrub-grass.

"How on earth did that happen?" Dan wondered.

The two got out of the Hummer and met Robert halfway.

"Did you hit something?" Bill asked him.

"No! It had been vibrating for quite a while. Then just a moment ago, it turned into a wobble, so I slowed down. I think you know the rest of the story."

Robert went to retrieve the tire, which was about fifteen feet away. Bill and Dan went to the front of the pickup to survey the damage.

"Everything looks pretty good actually, including the axel!" Bill reported, as Robert came back rolling the tire.

"It's a good thing you weren't going at full speed. It could have been the last drive you ever took," Bill remarked.

"I can't believe Jimmy missed that on the pre-trip inspection," Robert said in disbelief.

After jacking up the truck and replacing the tire, Robert moved it forward and back a few feet to test it out. He then stepped out.

"Well, apart from a little squeaking, it seems to be just fine," he reported.

He then began checking the lug-nuts on the other three tires.

"You guys should check your tires as well," he suggested.

After completing his walk-around, he stood up and waited for his companions to complete their checks. Bill ended at the front right wheel. He stood up while keeping his eyes looking downward. He then looked up at Robert, but didn't say anything.

"Is something wrong?" Robert wondered.

"You're never going to believe this," Bill responded very disappointedly. "These ones are all loose."

"What?" Robert remarked. "What are the chances of that? And on the same wheel too!"

"Did one of us say or do something to make Jimmy mad?" Bill wondered.

"I know *I* haven't. At least not yet," Robert threatened. "Jimmy is probably the top mechanic in the entire Southwest. This just doesn't make any sense."

Dan could picture the big hillbilly in his mind's eye. He knew *he* would never want to make him angry. The thought of someone from Eos maliciously trying to harm them, made them all very uncomfortable. Bill tightened everything up as they tried to figure out a rational explanation. None of them could come up with anything. Robert pointed out that they couldn't afford to waste any more precious time, and the three demoralized men took back to the road.

Fortunately, the rest of their trip was uneventful. Within three more hours, they had reached the Phoenix city limits. The two vehicles stopped in a short pull-out area by the side of the road. Led by Robert, the three quickly went over their strategy for the operation.

"What was that address again?" Robert asked, as he laid out a detailed map of the city over the hood of the hummer.

***

Helen was in the pantry retrieving a can of kidney beans. It was the second to last one on the shelf, and she worried about what her short-term future held in store, as she was quickly running out of food. At that moment, she heard knocking at the front door. Her very first instinct was to reach for her shotgun, which hadn't left her side since the visit by the phony city workman. After placing the can on the kitchen counter, she headed nervously for the door. As she cautiously made her way there, there was another knock; this time a little more forceful.

"Who is it?" she called out, trying to sound confident.

"Good morning!" a male voice answered. "We're looking for Helen Delshay. Are you familiar with that name?"

Helen looked through the peephole. She saw a rugged looking man in army fatigues. She could also make out that there were others with him.

"What do you need her for?" Helen demanded to know.

"I'm sorry, but it's personal business. I could only talk about that with her."

"I need some identification that shows you're really with the military!"

"Actually, we're not with the military."

"Who are you then?"

"It's a long story and we're in a bit of a rush ma'am. I understand your safety concerns, but it's a personal matter. One of Helen's relatives is looking for her."

"And who exactly would that be?"

"Her son ma'am."

"I don't have a son, but I do have a loaded shotgun!" she warned. Everyone on both sides of the door realized she had just given herself away. After a short spell of silence, the male visitor spoke again.

"That's because you gave him up for adoption, isn't that correct Helen?" he asked in a compassionate tone of voice.

There was no answer.

"Helen?"

"How do you know this?" she finally inquired.

Because he told me ma'am," the man divulged.

"And where is *he*?" Helen asked with a shaky voice.

"He's right here Helen."

"Tell him to stand close to the door!" she demanded nervously.

When she looked through the peephole again, she saw Dan staring at her like a deer in the headlights. After what seemed like forever to Dan, there was the sound of a deadbolt unlocking. It was followed by the click of the doorknob. Slowly, the door creaked open. As Bill and Robert looked on, Dan and his mother engaged in a silent staring contest. As Helen studied her son's face, tears began streaming down her cheeks. Normally, Dan was not easily moved to tears. However, he could feel his eyes well up as his vision became blurred with moisture.

"You have your father's lips," were Helen's first words to Dan; in over twenty years anyway.

From a near motionless state, she suddenly pounced on Dan, as she embraced him tightly and sobbed. Dan slowly lifted his arms up and around her. It wasn't as private a reunion as he would have hoped for. He felt rather self-conscious with the other two behind him. However, his uneasy discomfort was still tinged with a sense of satisfaction.

When she finally released Dan from her bear hug, she held him by both arms and admired him.

"You're so handsome and healthy looking. What's your name dear?"

"Daniel," he replied with a grin.

"That's a beautiful name," she gushed.

Of course, he could have said his name was Chopped Liver, and she still would have loved it.

"Please, come inside with your friends. There's so much to talk about."

She led the trio inside clutching Dan's hand, as if he were a schoolboy who might dart away unexpectedly.

For the next two hours Dan and Helen shared their condensed histories with each other. The first thing Helen wanted to know was how he had come to find her. As expected, the reason Helen opted for adoption was that Dan's father had just been killed in Iraq. She felt it would be a hardship for herself and her child to study or work full time, while raising that child alone. Not to mention that she was an emotional wreck at the time.

"I wanted you to be raised in a stable environment, with a mother and a father. And I just couldn't provide you with that. Giving you up was as hard as losing William. Those were the worst days of my life. I hope you can understand that, and forgive me someday," she pleaded.

"I already have," Dan assured her.

"Thank you," she sobbed, as she covered her heart with both hands.

What was a revelation to Dan was that his father was a Native American; of Navajo origin. His mother on the other hand, was of English descent. Dan felt this was what it must be like to recover from amnesia. He had finally discovered himself. He could now look people in the eye and say, 'this is who I am.' The fact that both his parents seemed like fine human beings, also came as a relief. His only lament was not having had a chance to meet his father, whose photo he was now holding.

"I can't believe how young you are. I was expecting you to be much older," Dan revealed.

"Well, I was still pretty young when I had you, but I'll take that as a compliment," she gushed.

Robert and Bill had quietly and patiently sat by the whole time, listening to the sometimes emotional exchange. Helen had supplied them with canned soda and peanuts; a lavish treat given her circumstances.

"I'm so sorry to have to interrupt you two," Robert suddenly blurted out. "However, we can't afford to stay here much longer. We have to use what time we have left to explain Eos to Helen."

"Explain *who*?" she asked curiously.

"Actually, it's more like a what and where," Dan pointed out.

As Dan and Bill briefed Helen on everything Eos, Robert went out back to make use of the latrine. After they'd gotten Helen up to speed on all the details, they told her about Chief Q's invitation. She was visibly overwhelmed, after so much drama in such a short time. But with the thought of losing her son again, albeit temporarily, she agreed to join them. Although he didn't tell her so, Dan would have made a heck of a fuss if she'd refused.

"Great!" Bill declared. "I'll go fill up the tanks. Dan, you should help your mother pack up a few essentials as quickly as you can."

"Just let me know what needs carrying and I'll be your mule," Robert offered, as everyone started moving about.

Bill hadn't been gone a minute, when he suddenly burst back in.

"The pickup's gone!" he yelled out angrily.

Robert took a few steps and looked out the door to the driveway. Maybe he hoped Bill was just pulling his leg.

"Damn! That's what I get for bringing my old bucket of bolts," Robert cursed as he came back into the living room.

"It's a good thing they didn't take the Hummer too," Dan opined. "We'd be stranded."

"No. The only way to steal that thing is to physically pick it up and carry it off somehow," Robert explained. "Although if we stay around here long enough, I can see that happening. Let's get a move on everybody!" he ordered with two claps.

While everyone else was busy packing, Bill returned from the driveway.

"You wouldn't shoot the messenger, would you Robert?" he asked with an unsettling seriousness.

Robert put down the suitcase he was carrying and stopped in his tracks.

"What is it now?" he said with a look that conveyed his apprehension.

"The gas cans are empty," Bill replied bleakly.

"What do you mean empty?" Robert asked incredulously.

"Empty...as in...un-full."

"But we haven't used them yet. And I was the one who filled those myself last night!"

"Well," said Bill, "my guess is that the person who loosened our wheels for us, is probably the one who sabotaged our fuel supply as well."

"I knew Jimmy couldn't have been that negligent," Robert declared. "Whoever did this, did it on purpose. Unfortunately, the fact remains that someone at Eos doesn't want us coming back any time soon."

Dan was coming down the stairs and only overheard Robert's last words.

"What? Who doesn't want us coming back?"

"We're not sure," said Robert. "Whoever emptied our gas cans."

"What? How are we supposed to get back?" Dan worried.

"We'll try to find an open gas station," Bill suggested.

"Didn't you notice the two we passed on the way here?" Robert quizzed him. Bill gave him a blank stare as a response. "They both had signs that said 'More fuel in two days'. And one of them already had a queue forming," Robert informed him. "How much fuel was left in the tank when you got here?"

"Just over a third of a tank," Bill replied.

"Okay, so it took just under two thirds to get here," Robert calculated. "Rather than take a risk, and drive around aimlessly looking for gas, we need to head straight home."

Bill and Dan both looked confused. Bill spoke for the two of them;

"But how can we make it back on less than what it took to get here?"

"I have a plan. Give me your vests guys," Robert said as he took his off. At that moment, Helen came down the stairs.

"Is everything all right down here? You guys are chattier than my neighbor Marilyn," she teased.

"Mrs. Delshay, would you happen to have any tools around?" Robert asked her. "I seem to have misplaced mine, along with my truck."

"First of all, you can call me Helen. And yes, there are a whole bunch of tools in that closet over there. They were William's, and I couldn't part with them, even though I don't know what half of them are for," she admitted.

As Robert opened the closet, he noticed toolboxes immediately.

"There's gotta be a wire cutter in here somewhere. You guys keep loading up as I work on the Hummer!" he commanded his troops.

When Dan saw Robert duct-taping the solar vests to the sides and back of the vehicle, his curiosity was piqued.

"I thought *those* were solar panels on top?"

"They are, but you would need a solar panel four times the size of this Hummer, to run this baby on solar power alone. The technology just isn't there yet," Robert told him.

"So, what's the purpose in using them at all then?"

"Well, they do provide some extra fuel efficiency, together with the kinetic energy system and whatever other ingenious tweaks our engineer came up with. Otherwise, you'd have made it about halfway here before needing to refuel. If I can hook these vests up to the existing panels, that'll give us a little boost. Then I'll disable the daytime running lights and make sure to keep the air-con off the whole time."

"Will that enable us to make it back?" Dan inquired.

"I'm hoping. If not all the way, it should at least bring us really close."

"Then what," Dan pressed.

"Then that's where these fancy hiking shoes of ours would come in handy. Which reminds me, you should tell your mother to pack something comfy, but sturdy," Robert advised.

"I'm on it," Dan responded, thinking to himself how odd it still was to hear the phrase, 'your mother.'

By the time everything was loaded, and Robert had successfully hooked up the vests to the solar pack, it was already one forty-five in the afternoon. The plan had been to leave by one o'clock at the latest.

"All right, everybody on board! We can't afford to waste another minute!" Robert hollered.

Bill rode shotgun with Robert, while Dan and Helen sat in the back. The two had a lot to catch up on, and a lot of time to do it now. But they hadn't even driven out of the neighborhood yet, when Dan suddenly hollered at the driver.

"Robert! Stop here for a second!"

Robert pulled to the side while responding to Dan's demand.

"What is it?" he asked rather impatiently.

Something outside had caught Dan's eye.

"I'll be right back!" he said, opening the door.

"Wait!" Robert yelled, to no avail.

"It's okay, I got this," Bill said as he followed Dan to the front yard of a house, a few feet behind the Hummer.

As he quickly strode into the open yard, a group of three kids sprinted away down the street, leaving a younger one behind. He was about nine years old and was sitting on the lawn crying.

"Are you okay?" Dan asked him as he approached.

The child didn't speak. He only nodded yes through his sobbing.

"What did they do to you?" Dan inquired.

"Th...they stole my candy-bar," the boy said as he wiped his tears away. Dan extended his hand to him and pulled him off the ground.

"Hold on a second, I'll be right back," Dan promised him.

He quickly ran back to the car and grabbed his backpack from the back seat.

"What are you doing?" Robert demanded. "We have to leave, *now*!"

"This won't take long," Dan answered with an irritating calmness, as his mother looked on silently.

Bill could see exactly what was unfolding. He also said nothing, as he scanned the area for any signs of danger. Dan unzipped the bag as he marched back to the yard.

"I don't have any candy-bars, but do you like peanuts?" he asked the boy.

"Yes."

"I also have some gum."

"Cool," the child responded. As he received the goodies, he questioned his donor. "Do you know when the lights are going to come back?"

"I wish I knew the answer to that. Why? You're not afraid of the dark are you?"

"Sometimes," the boy answered, somewhat embarrassed.

"Well this is your lucky day," Dan said, pulling his flashlight out of the backpack. "Here's a present for you. It's a special flashlight, like the ones the Army uses. It's small, but very powerful. You can light up the whole house with it."

"Wow! Thanks!" The kid's eyes lit up as he turned it over in his hand.

"Where's your mom or dad anyway? Are you alone here?" Dan finally asked him.

"No. My mom went to the bathroom. She'll be back soon."

"Well, you really should stay inside the house while you wait for her. As you can see, there are some bad people around." Dan cautioned.

"Okay, I will. Thanks for all the stuff."

"You're welcome," Dan said as he waved and turned toward Bill.

The two quickly walked back to the waiting vehicle. As the young boy was headed indoors, his mother came out through the front door.

"What's going on out here?" she asked concernedly.

Her son excitedly rattled off the history of the preceding moments. Before closing the car door, Dan turned around to see the kid and his mother both waving. Turning to Helen, Dan noticed her wiping a tear from her eye.

"What's wrong?" he wondered.

"Oh, nothing's wrong. You just remind me so much of your father."

"I can't fault your compassion son," Robert declared, "but we can't be stopping along the way to help anyone unless it's an emergency."

"I thought that was the whole purpose of Eos, to train us to help society," Dan protested.

"Well, it is. But we have to get *ourselves* set up properly first, with a solid foundation. For example, right now we have a bad apple in our midst." Robert reminded him.

"That reminds me," Dan said excitedly. "I know who might be the saboteur."

"Who?" Robert asked keenly.

"Johnny, the hermit," Dan proposed.

"But how could he have made it past the cameras?" Bill objected.

"I'm not sure. Maybe he got lucky and no one was watching at that moment. But the vehicles were out in the driveway overnight, so it's a strong possibility. He's the only person I can think of who might want to do something like that," Dan insisted. "He thinks Chad is King Herod, but I'm slowly gaining his trust. The next time I see him, I'll try to find out if he's behind this."

"Well it sounds a bit sophisticated for him, but then again, we shouldn't underestimate anyone. I'll scour the vicinity of the driveway later for dumped fuel. It's our duty to keep everyone at Eos safe," Robert avowed.

"When we get back, we need to get to the bottom of this. And we may have to overhaul our security procedures," he added.

***

Since smoking was prohibited inside Eos, Chad had gone for a stroll just outside the perimeter of the property. At the same time, he was also doing the rounds, scanning the environs for any suspicious activities. After every few steps, he would stop and suck in a dose of the white smoke. It was during one of these pauses that something caught his eye. Behind some dense foliage, he spotted brown fur. He calmly threw down the cigarette and snuffed it out with his foot. He reached behind his back and slid out an arrow, which he paired with the bow that was slung over his shoulder. After pulling the shaft back all the way to the arrowhead, he took aim at his target. He then carefully walked around to the side of the bush to confront his prey. He hoped it was something big enough to roast, but not so big as to require more than one arrow. If that were the case, he could always use his sidearm to finish the job. When he was no more than fifteen feet away from his quarry, his prey suddenly leapt out into the open. Chad flinched and almost released the projectile.

"Herod!" Johnny yelled out at the top of his lungs.

"What the hell?" Chad exclaimed, still holding his aim. "So, we finally meet!"

"I've been watching you Herod!" Johnny ranted. "I know you've been unfaithful!"

"You're totally insane," Chad declared, rather calmly.

Johnny wouldn't let up. He pointed an accusatory finger directly at Chad.

"When my cousin gets here, you're going to be in biiiiiig trouble!" he warned.

Those were the last words he would ever speak.

Chapter Eleven

And the Oscar Goes to...

Having already reached the open highway, the Hummer was gliding along on cruise control. Robert had made sure to avoid any jack-rabbit starts on the way through town, desperately trying to economize on their precious fuel supply.

"Oh, you gotta be kidding!" Robert whined.

"What is it?" Dan asked.

"There's a police roadblock up ahead," he replied.

It wasn't much of a roadblock, just one car, but it was parked right in the middle of the highway.

"Those might not be cops," Dan cautioned.

"What do you mean," Bill asked.

"Eve and I were chased by a couple of guys in a police car in this area. Except, we don't think they were legit."

As Robert slowed down, Dan craned his neck from the back seat to get a better look.

"I didn't get a good look at them earlier, but it looks like the same car."

"Roll up all the windows," Robert ordered. "I'll pull up to them and see who they are and what they want."

As he rolled up to the patrol car, he had his window open just a crack. The two men standing there were in civilian clothes.

"Good afternoon!" Robert greeted them confidently.

"Roll down your window!" the taller one demanded.

"I can hear you just fine actually!" Robert replied politely.

The man then reached for the gun in his shoulder holster. Seeing this, Robert drove off immediately, with a shot bouncing off his side window. The two men kept shooting at them, as they drove around the patrol-car and away. It was a waste of bullets however, as all their shots hit the armored body of the Hummer.

"Oh my goodness!" Helen gasped. "They almost got you Robert!"

"No, the windows are bullet resistant as well as the rest of the vehicle, except for the tires. Thank goodness they missed those."

Robert quickly turned his head to the left to check the damage on his side window. There was a big white circle around the point of impact. From the inside, it looked as though someone had hurled a large snowball at him.

"Yeah, those *must* be the same guys," Dan assumed.

"Sorry Mrs. Delshay," Robert empathized. "You must be wondering if it was such a good idea to come with us."

Helen exchanged her serious expression for a content grin.

"There's no place in the world I'd rather be right now," she said, as she clasped Dan's hand.

***

Chad walked up to the gate, by the intercom buzzer, and started speaking loudly.

"I need both of you to meet me at the main entrance ASAP!" he requested adamantly.

"*Who's going to watch the monitors Chad?*"

"It's okay, it'll only take a couple of minutes."

"*Alright Chad, we'll be up there as soon as we can.*"

"Incompetent morons," Chad mumbled, as he fumbled for the small remote control attached to his keychain.

After the gate slid open, he took a quick look around the front yard. He then put his thumb and ring finger to his mouth, and emitted a sharp, loud whistle. Three men with semi-automatic weapons came running through the open gateway; two Caucasians and one African-American, all wearing regular civilian clothing. They suddenly stopped in front of Chad, awaiting further instructions.

"All right. As soon as we get inside, the two of you take your positions. Mark and I will take care of the rest. Anyone tries to get in or out…cap 'em," Chad instructed. "As soon as we've set up shop, we'll let you know through the P.A. system."

The three thugs followed Chad, as he quickly led them through the house to the back yard. At the very back where the main entrance was located, he stopped. He aimed his weapon at the big doors, and his henchmen followed suit. After a few short moments, they heard some tinkering sounds coming from inside. They all lifted their guns, which had by then sagged, to upper body levels. Needless to say, when the pair of guardians opened the doors, they were utterly stunned.

"Chad, what's going on?" one of them ventured timidly.

"I believe this is what they call a hostile takeover," Chad taunted them. "I need you to place all your weapons on the ground, including knives, bows and arrows."

After the small pile of weapons had been gathered up, Chad entered, and began descending down the stairway.

"Follow me gentlemen. Last one in, make sure you close the door behind you."

The two now helpless guardians were led back in behind Chad.

Everyone in the complex was winding down their daily duties and preparing for dinner. Eve however, was at her busiest, setting the tables for the first dinner shift. Holding a pile of napkins, she stopped in her tracks when the P.A. system came alive.

"*Attention all residents, attention all residents! This is Commander Chad, with an important announcement!*"

She grinned and shook her head at Chad's playful introduction.

"There is going to be a general meeting in the cafeteria in thirty minutes. All residents please report to the cafeteria for an important meeting!"

"In the cafeteria?" Eve exclaimed.

She wondered why no one had informed her sooner. And how would everyone fit in here at the same time? As if to answer her directly, Chad continued;

"my helpers and I will be there momentarily to fold up the tables."

Eve couldn't believe the timing. What was so important, for them to have to interrupt everyone's dinner like this?

All around Eos, people wondered the same thing. The optimists figured life on the outside had returned to normal, while the pessimists all feared the worst.

No one was more surprised than Chief Q. He was in the library reading poetry when he heard the announcement. He couldn't understand how there could be a general meeting without his okay, let alone without him even knowing about it. After all, he was the official leader of the entire project. He also didn't see Chad's use of the term 'commander' as very playful. Normally Chief Q *was* an optimist. But right now, he was among those fearing the worst. He arose from the small table and folded his reading glasses. After tucking them inside their case, he picked up the book, and slid it back into its home slot on the shelf. As Miss Jenkins saw him pass by, she solicited him for any details.

"Chief, what's this meeting all about?"

"Your guess is as good as mine. I'll see you at the pow-wow."

She was quite surprised by his seeming lack of awareness. After checking the four aisles in the room, making sure they were all unoccupied, she turned off the lights and headed for the meeting as well.

Inside the cafeteria, Chad stood at the front of the room near the kitchen, while his right-hand man Mark stood at the entrance, frisking everyone who came along. Both had their weapons in their hands, which was not a comforting sight for those entering. The two guardians meanwhile, had been turned into unwilling volunteers. They were the ones who had folded up the tables and placed them against the walls.

Chief Q was one of the first to enter. He looked at Mark silently as he came in. The elder leader appeared unintimidated by the large man with the Slavic features. After being frisked by the strange new face, Chief Q gave him a piece of his mind.

"If you ever touch me like that again, you better be buying me dinner after."

Although his words were humorous, his expression was anything but.

"Yeah, I heard about your cheesy wisecracks. Just move along Injun." Chief Q ignored the taunting and walked over to Chad. He noticed Eve talking with Michael over to his right. From the concerned look on their faces, he could tell they weren't discussing the menu options. He looked Chad square in the eyes as he approached.

"Can you please explain to me exactly what's happening here?" he asked sternly.

"Sorry, but I don't have time to speak to everyone individually. You'll have to wait 'til the gangs all here."

Chad said this so lackadaisically that it absolutely infuriated Chief Q. The warrior in him wanted to physically subdue Chad, but the peacemaker in him knew that could lead to bloodshed. For the sake of the others, if no one else, he managed to control his passions. Without saying another word, he looked over to where Michael and Eve were standing. The other two guardians had now joined them, after completing their assigned tasks.

"What is going on here fellows?" Chief Q asked with frustration.

"Chad's taking over, and he's got three guys helping him," answered the one on the left in a hushed tone.

"It's our fault Sir," added his partner. "We let him trick us into leaving the security room. They ambushed us and took all our weapons. They're guarding the entrance into Eos."

"Are you both uninjured?" the concerned Chief inquired.

They both nodded yes.

"That's all that matters at this point."

"What will happen when the others get back?" Eve asked with visible anxiety.

"Well, they didn't hurt these two. There's no reason for them to hurt the others either."

"I hope you're right," Eve replied nervously.

As they had been speaking, people had continued trickling in steadily. They would then cluster together in groups and start exchanging rumors and theories. So much so, that Chad became irritated by it.

"Alright! Since everyone seems to have started without me, we'll just commence this meeting a few minutes early then!"

A sudden hush came over the crowd as they all turned toward Chad, who was soon accompanied by Mark.

"I don't have a microphone, so everyone listen up good! We're not trying to take over your precious little paradise here! We just want the loot, then we'll be out of your hair! All you batty people can then go back to your regular cave duties!"

"What loot?" Michael cried out. "We didn't exactly come in here carrying Mona Lisas under our arms! All we have is just some personal jewellery!"

"What do you take me for? A petty thief?" Chad answered him. "I'm not after your little trinkets! I'm talking about the motherlode!"

Everyone seemed confused. Some began to whisper amongst themselves.

"Don't you people know simple math? Look...Katzman was a billionaire! He left a good chunk of his fortune to this endeavour! He obviously wouldn't leave it in some bank account, where it could be devalued or frozen if there was a financial breakdown! It only makes sense that he would put it into gold and/or jewels! And where would be a secure yet accessible place to stash it?"

"You think there's buried treasure around here?" Michael asked incredulously. "*I've* never heard anything about that!"

"Why would you? You're not the Chief caretaker, are you?" Chad pointed out.

Chad then turned toward Chief Q who was standing a few feet in front of him, and smiled.

"I'm sure Q knows what I'm talking about though. Don't you Chief?"

His probing question drew no response from the caretaker. Eve on the other hand, couldn't keep quiet.

"Just promise not to hurt the others when they return! Take whatever you can find and leave us all in peace!"

"You're assuming they'll be *able* to return." Chad remarked casually.

A blank look came over Eve's face.

"What is *that* supposed to mean?" she asked apprehensively.

"It seems that someone tampered with their wheels before they left!" Chad bragged with a devilish grin.

The thought of any harm coming to Dan was more than she could bear. With a half yell, half growl, she lunged forward at Chad with fire in her eyes. She was met with a hard, backhanded slap to the face. She had barely hit the ground, when she picked herself right back up. Ignoring the stinging pain on the left side of her face, she went in for a second attempt. This time, Chad swung his assault rifle to his left, and cracked her on the side of the head with it. Eve immediately crumpled in a heap. She was down for the count.

"Feisty one!" Chad remarked.

Seeing this, Michael and a few other men got all wild-eyed and began moving forward. On cue, the two gunmen turned their weapons toward the crowd.

"Anymore heroes?" Chad asked threateningly, holding up his rifle with his right hand, while caressing a hand grenade in his belt with the left.

"Enough!" Chief Q yelled out, as he brought his hand up to Michael's chest and nudged him back.

"Hey, the ball's in your court old man! Just tell us where the stash is and we'll be history!" Chad negotiated.

"I will die before I ever betray this mission." Chief Q stated heroically.

"That's what I expected from a brainwashed idealist like yourself! However, I also expect that you wouldn't be so willing to give up *her* life!" Chad said confidently, as he pointed his gun at Eve's helpless body.

Chief Q offered no reply as everyone looked on silently. He then stepped forward slowly.

"That's more like it!" Chad said with a grin.

But he quickly changed his tune, as Chief Q just kept coming.

"Okay, that's far enough!" he warned.

Strangely, Chief Q continued to move toward him calmly and silently, until he was within touching distance. He then grabbed Chad's gun with both hands.

"Have you completely lost your mind?" Chad asked in disbelief.

Then, in almost comical fashion, the elder leader began to try and wrest the weapon from Chad's sweaty hands. The more Chad tightened his grip, the more Chief Q intensified his efforts.

"You're pretty strong for an old man!" Chad muttered through gritted teeth.

In fact, the determined caretaker seemed to be gaining the upper hand, as everyone watched on in utter amazement. When it became quite clear that Chad was about to lose the battle, a few quick rounds of ammo spat out of mark's weapon directly into Chief Q's back. After a quick spasm, his lifeless body fell forward like a felled tree, as everyone either gasped or screamed in horror.

"What have you done? You imbecile!" Chad screamed at his partner furiously. "Now how are we supposed to find the stuff?"

"But he looked like he was winning!" Mark protested.

"That's exactly what he wanted you to do, you idiot! Don't you have an ounce of intelligence in that thick skull of yours? Didn't you see how I handled that bitch? You could have done the same thing!"

"Sorry Chad," Mark apologized shamefully. "Maybe he left instructions somewhere, in case something happened to him," he added hopefully.

"You better hope so! In the meantime, we'll have to move on to plan B!"

"There's a plan B?" mark asked with a confused look.

"There is now, thanks to you!"

Raising his voice even higher, Chad addressed the crowd.

"Everyone here is gonna look for the loot! Every forty-eight hours that passes without us finding it, means the death penalty for one of you! Oh, and if any of you are contemplating leaving in the middle of the night; there will be someone stationed at the entrance and in the monitor room, twenty-four seven. For every person that escapes, another will pay with their life! So, I suggest we all work together here for a happy ending!"

He then turned toward his less competent counterpart.

"You go look in this old man's quarters for any clues about the funds!"

"Yes sir," Mark answered docilely.

Chad looked down at Chief Q.

"Someone get some plastic tarp and wrap him up! Stick him in the walk-in freezer for now! The rest of you all get busy and start searching! This meeting is adjourned!"

Father James and the rabbi came forward from out of the horrified crowd. Rabbi Yosef knelt down and checked Chief Q's pulse. After a few seconds, he looked up at Father James and shook his head sadly. The two then went over to Eve. The priest slid his hands under her shoulders and lifted her.

"Let's get her over to the clinic," he said to Rabbi Yosef, who immediately grabbed her legs and helped him carry Eve away.

"What are *you* staring at?" Chad said to Michael, as everyone else began exiting in quiet shock.

"What happened to you?" Michael blurted. "How did you change so much since I first met you?"

"The only thing that's changed is your perception of me, I assure you."

"I can't understand how you passed the selection process and all the tests." Michael stated with awe.

"Hey, I'm a car salesman remember? Although, I did such a fine job of convincing you, that maybe *acting* was my true calling," Chad boasted.

"You even returned the wallet. How could you possibly know it was a test?" Michael wondered.

"I didn't. You see, my philosophy has always been to use a small catch as bait for bigger fish. My intention was to sell you a car the next time you needed one. It's little tricks like that, which made me the number two car dealer in the state of Illinois," Chad bragged. "When I brought you the wallet, and you started going on about this project, you got my curiosity up. When you had finished your little spiel, I figured Eos would make a nice insurance policy if the shit ever hit the fan. Then I found out that Katzman was Chief Q's sugar-daddy. Well, you can't land a bigger fish than that. He was a freakin' blue whale. Anyway, are you gonna stand here and make small talk all day? Or are you gonna help us find where the goose laid his golden eggs?"

As Chief Q's lifeless corpse was being wrapped up by two other residents, Michael quietly began making his way to the door. But not before turning to give Chad a death-stare first. Chad smiled back and taunted him with a cute little wave, which only served to further incense an already livid Michael. As he left the room, he was feeling just about every emotion possible. In addition to the obvious anger and disgust, he was also in mourning for his chief caretaker, and personal friend. He felt guilt, for not having screened out the likes of Chad, and he also felt a sense of urgency in finding any valuables before anyone else got hurt; not to mention anxiety over what would become of Eos once its supplies were exhausted, if they did find any treasure.

***

With the late afternoon sun behind them, Helen and the three guardians found themselves about two hours shy of Eos.

"Well guys...I think we have no choice but to call it a day," Robert announced.

"What do you mean?" Bill inquired.

"The sun's not very intense anymore. Any solar power we're getting right now is minimal. If we keep driving, I guarantee we're done inside of one hour. We need to pull into the rest stop up ahead, and bunk down for the night. In the morning, we can make our final run. If we still come up short, it should just take a bit of a hike to make up the difference."

"Do we have a tent in the back?" Bill asked.

"No, we'll have to sleep right here. Helen can have the back seat to herself. The three of us will rotate in the front seats. We'll each take a four-hour shift on guard duty."

"I'll scout a spot for a campfire, if Ranger Rob will permit me," Bill offered.

"Just keep the fire extinguisher handy. We don't want to be responsible for a brushfire," Robert advised.

When darkness began to envelop them, they lit the pile of wood and dry grass in the fire-pit they'd made. Bill had offered to stay awake first. He boiled some water over the fire to make instant coffee. As Robert got a blanket out for Helen, Dan stood between the campfire and the Hummer, gazing up at the endlessly clear sky. Far from the city lights, the stars began to come alive as the sun's influence diminished. Dan couldn't help but be in awe of the universe, like so many before him down through the millennia.

Without putting his thoughts into actual word form, he concocted a sort of informal prayer in his mind. He thought about how much his life had changed in the past few weeks, mostly for the better in his opinion, despite all the chaos around him. He felt gratitude for that, but apprehension about the possible breach of security back at the caves. He still hoped that somehow it was all just an unfortunate chain of events. Earlier, he had untied Chief Q's feather from his backpack. He'd formed a loop with the leather strap, and placed it around his neck. As he now held it between his fingers, he hoped that everyone at Eos was fine, especially Eve.

As he remembered what Chief Q had said, Dan chuckled to himself. Since it was already dark, he assumed owls would be the ones to carry his prayer up to Heaven. He looked around discreetly to make sure no one was watching him. He then lifted the feather up above his forehead, and held it for a few seconds against the backdrop of twinkling stars.

Chapter Twelve

Worst Case Scenario

Inside the clinic, as Susan pulled back the white bedsheet, the priest and the rabbi lay Eve down carefully. She had a swollen left cheek, and Susan lifted her hair back to reveal a nasty bump above that.

"I'll take an x-ray to see if there's a fracture," she said.

After doing so, she discovered there was probably no fracture. Eve had however, suffered a substantial concussion.

"We don't have an MRI here, and I can't tell conclusively from the x-ray, if there's any bleeding in the brain. Her vital signs are stable, which is a good sign. But if she doesn't regain consciousness very soon and her condition worsens, then we'll have to assume there's a hematoma."

"Then what would you do?" Rabbi Yosef asked hesitantly, not knowing what a hematoma even was.

"Well, it would be the doctor's final decision, but we would have to release the pressure by surgical means," the nurse said somberly. "Would either of you be able to help watch over her?"

"Yes, of course," responded the rabbi.

"I'd be happy to as well," Father James concurred.

"Great, we'll take turns. This machine here monitors her vital signs."

She then proceeded to instruct the pair on what to look out for.

"If she wakes up or if her condition worsens, come get me or Doctor Monroe right away. I'm sure my husband would be willing to take a shift as well," she said of Ken, the dentist.

***

Dan was responsible for the third and final security shift. This enabled him to watch day-break over the mountains. He took in a deep breath of the cool morning air, and then a sip of his coffee. In the dawn silence, he felt like he had a private screening of the fiery, red sunrise. He suddenly remembered his earlier conversation with Bill the day before, about missing out on the previous dawn. He could now understand exactly what all the fuss was about.

As he took another sip of his instant java, he noticed a Dusky Grouse scurrying into a tree through the corner of his eye. He wasn't sure what type of bird it was, but this gave him an idea.

He put down his metal mug and set up his bow and arrow. Stealthily moving his way toward the tree, he pulled the bow string back tightly. As soon as the bird emerged again, Dan's arrow swooshed against his tail feathers. Of course, this only served to startle his prey, which quickly disappeared into a nearby ravine, as Dan reached behind his back for another arrow. He knew they had only crackers, nuts, and dried fruits for breakfast, having eaten all the beef jerky the night before. He was hoping to surprise the others with some sort of roasted protein. He pulled the arrow back and quietly rotated in place, hoping for a second chance.

He didn't have to wait very long; another Dusky Grouse, an even larger one, quickly emerged. He patiently waited for it to slow its pace, keeping it in his line of fire. As soon as it stopped to check for some berries, it was skewered, by Dan's homemade projectile. From a distance of roughly twenty-five feet, it hit with enough force to go almost right through the bird. Dan was glad he got a clean shot in, so the unfortunate fowl didn't have to suffer very long. After a quick convulsion, it was laying lifelessly on the rocky terrain.

It wasn't until Dan had removed the arrow from his catch, that he realized he didn't know how to pluck and eviscerate poultry. Luckily for him, Robert was an early riser.

"What have we here?" Robert asked from behind, startling Dan a bit.

"Oh, I just caught this bird and I wanted to use it for our breakfast. There's just one problem."

"What's that?" Robert wondered.

"I have no idea what I'm doing," Dan confessed with a chuckle.

"Well, first of all, kudos on downing a Dusky Grouse," Robert congratulated him. They're extremely hard to nab. If you miss the first time, you won't get a second chance."

"Actually," Dan admitted, "this was my second target. The first one disappeared into the ravine."

"You're lucky you weren't using a rifle. Every single one of them within earshot would have left the state. You must have natural archery skills to be pulling this off though, with such little training."

"Thanks, but maybe I just got lucky," Dan suggested modestly.

"Maybe," Robert concurred with a shrug. "You're in luck however. I *do* know how to dress a bird, and I don't mean in a cute little outfit either," he joked, much to Dan's amusement. "I'll show you how it's done, so you know for next time."

Within roughly two hours, the grouse had been plucked, gutted, washed, halved, and roasted over the campfire. After having breakfast, the foursome chatted while waiting for the sun to gain intensity. Helen was catching up on Dan's evolving relationship with Eve.

"That reminds me. Would you happen to have five dollars I could borrow?" Dan asked her with a grin.

"I think I do," she replied as she pulled her handbag around.

Just then, Robert stood up and announced it was time to leave. It was just shy of high noon.

"I'll have to explain as we drive," Dan told his mother, as she slid a bill out from her purse.

As they approached the hilly terrain leading to Eos, the vehicle began to jerk and sputter. The occupants shared a collective groan.

"Ohhh...and we were so close too," Robert whined as he coasted over to the shoulder of the road.

"Okay, so we're about a two-hour hike away. We'll only need to bring our packs and a little extra water with us. Once we get home, I'll bring a jerry-can back here and pick up the Hummer. Bill, if you could give me a ride back here later, I'd appreciate it."

"No problem," Bill replied.

After quickly packing up their personal items, they walked in single file along the side of the highway, with Robert up front. The three men wore their camo sport caps, while Helen enjoyed the shade underneath her oversized white hat.

Within an hour, they had turned onto a dusty dirt road, on the last leg of their journey. Unfortunately, Helen wasn't at the same fitness level as her escorts. They had to constantly stop and wait, in order to allow her to remain close.

"That's odd," Robert blurted after removing his sunglasses.

"What is?" Bill asked.

"These tire tracks are rather new, and they don't match any of our vehicles."

The other three all looked down. Helen couldn't see much of anything, as Bill and Dan studied the faint patterns. Dan was the one who finally expressed what they were all thinking;

"Who do you think made them?"

"I'm not sure, but I guess we'll find out soon enough," was Robert's less than reassuring reply.

Further ahead, near the main footpath leading to the refuge, Robert stopped once again. This time he crouched down and inspected the ground very closely. They could all see what he was looking at so intently.

"Is that blood?" Dan asked apprehensively.

"I'm afraid so," Robert said, as he picked up a mottled piece of fur, with a stick he had found close by. "Does this look familiar to you?"

Dan leaned in for a closer look.

"That looks like a piece of Johnny's outfit!" Dan exclaimed in horror.

"I wonder if he injured himself," Bill proposed.

Without saying a word, Robert followed the trail of bloodstained ground leading to his right. In a small clearing between a few trees, he stopped. There was a mound of gravelly soil, which looked quite unnatural. He looked around for a bigger stick. Not having found one to his liking, he walked over to a tree and broke off a sturdy branch. In the meantime, the other three had followed him and now stood around him, watching intently.

Robert went back to the bumpy patch of soil and began to dig. At first, he stabbed at the ground briskly, trying to get as deep as possible in the shortest amount of time. Within moments however, he slowed right down to a careful clawing motion. He had hit the shaft of a wooden arrow. After carefully examining it, he dug further until he found the source of the furry material. Underneath it of course, was human flesh. He immediately stopped probing and began to replace the soil he'd removed.

"It's Johnny, isn't it?" Dan asked, although he pretty much already knew the answer to that question.

"Well, unless there was someone else who shared his fashion preferences, I think we can make that assumption without any further digging. What bothers me even more, is that he was killed with one of my arrows."

"What?" Bill exclaimed. "Are you sure?"

"There's no doubt. My handmade arrows have certain unique characteristics." Robert confirmed.

"But that would mean it was a guardian," Bill protested.

"I'm afraid so. And whoever it is, has brought in outsiders," Robert added.

"This means the others are in danger!" Dan cried out anxiously, as he suddenly bolted in the direction of the caves.

"Wait!" Robert barked with an authoritative tone. "We can't just go barging in there!"

Dan did indeed stop, as he awaited instructions from his leader.

"They must realize that one or more of us might be coming back. They're sure to be monitoring the entrance. We need to make a plan of action. We don't know exactly who's in on it, how many there are, or what their motives are. We need to gather some intel before we can attempt anything."

"How are we going to do that without getting inside?" Dan wondered, out loud.

"I think I know how to get inside without them knowing," Robert divulged. "The very first thing we need to do though, is to take care of your mother," he gestured toward Helen. "I remember you mentioning that Johnny lived in a little cave around here."

"Yeah, it's right on the side of that cliff over there," Dan pointed behind Bill.

"Okay, you take her there. Me and Bill will head for Eos," Robert dictated.

"Actually..." Dan protested, "I'd rather go with *you*. Bill could take her to the cliff instead. I can't just stand around waiting, not knowing if Eve's okay or not."

Robert thought to himself silently, while glancing at each of them. Finally, he nodded subtly in agreement.

"Okay...but you have to promise me you'll do exactly as I say."

"I will," Dan avowed eagerly, a little surprised that Robert had agreed to his request.

"Let's do this then," Robert said impatiently.

"You be careful, I don't want to lose you again," Helen implored Dan, as she embraced him.

"Don't worry Ma'am, I'll guard him with my life," Robert declared convincingly. "One of us will come back for you two as soon as it's safe to do so."

***

Helen's foot slid on some loose rocks, forcing her to break her fall with her hands.

"Are you okay?" Bill asked as he turned around.

"Yes, I'm fine," she replied as she stopped and rubbed her hands.

Bill had been trying to stabilize a path for her leading up to the cave. Even still, it was very steep and treacherous. There was only so much he could do. And this was the only accessible part of the cliff. He could only imagine how rough it must have been originally, before Johnny had beaten a path to his cliff dwelling. When they reached the small round opening, and entered, they were both pleasantly surprised. The tight entrance betrayed the actual size of the spacious abode behind it.

"Not too shabby for a hole in the wall," Bill declared. "Too bad he chose to become a hermit. Johnny had some serious sculpting skills," he added, admiring the hand-chiseled stone furniture. "Looks like he took a page out of the Flintstones book of interior decorating. It was also quite the engineering feat to bring up these pieces of rock."

"It's a shame he was killed like that," Helen lamented. "Is there no peaceful place left to be found *anywhere*?"

"Not in this world, I'm afraid," Bill replied bluntly, before putting his backpack down on a small sandstone table.

***

"So how exactly do you plan on getting inside with no one seeing you?" Dan couldn't help but wonder. "Through the underground parking lot maybe?" he guessed.

"No, that doesn't connect to the caverns. It's man-made, and self-enclosed. However, I know of a small opening above the underground river. If we can enlarge it enough for me to fit through, we're in business," Robert disclosed.

Having walked for the last few minutes along fairly level terrain, the two now came to inclining grounds.

"About halfway down the other side of this hill is where I saw the opening," Robert said as he pointed.

When they reached their destination, Robert began looking around hopefully.

"There it is!" he remarked excitedly.

He got down on all fours and put his ear to the rocky crevice.

"Yep, this is it. I can hear the river down below."

For his part, Dan wasn't sharing the enthusiasm. He was actually quite disappointed. If he didn't know about Robert's gifted skillset, he would've been surprised that he had even discovered this. It was really nothing more than a crack in the rocks. Robert quickly pulled out a small pry-bar from his backpack. With it, he began to scratch away at the loose dirt and gravel around the opening. He managed to isolate some of the smaller rocks and boulders. With his bare hands, he was able to remove some of the smaller, looser ones. With Dan's help, he dislodged one rock about the size of his head.

The opening was now big enough for a large poodle to squeeze through. Using one of the palm-sized rocks nearby, Robert chiseled away at the hole with the pry-bar. He wondered if it would put up with the abuse long enough to make some headway. Also, he hoped there was no one below to notice the goings on. At least, no one hostile to such activity.

Fortunately, the sandstone chipped away rather easily. With a denser rock type, his efforts would surely have been futile. However, it was still long and tedious work. And just when it looked like he would succeed, the pry-bar snapped right in half. The makeshift chisel just wasn't thick enough to withstand the abuse.

"Damn it!" Robert cursed, as the bottom piece fell through the opening with a muted clang.

"I hope that's big enough for me to squeeze through."

He put down the broken tool and the rock, and removed his holster.

"Can you get the para-cord out of your backpack?" he asked his young recruit.

"Sure," Dan complied.

Robert quickly tied his and Dan's cords together. He then started twisting the two to form one intertwined rope. He looped one end of the rope around a large nearby boulder.

"Okay, here's what I need you to do," Robert instructed him. "If I can fit through, lower my holster down to me."

"Will do," Dan replied, as Robert lowered the rope through the crevice.

He then pulled about five feet's worth of line, and looped it around his right ankle.

"When you see the rope loosen, pull it up, unwind it, and tie the two together. Tie my backpack to one end and wait for my signal; a sharp whistle or two. There's a pen and paper and a flashlight in there. I'll send up any info I get along with instructions. While you're waiting, build yourself a fire."

Sitting down in the hole with his lower legs inserted, he slowly lowered his knees and thighs, while supporting himself with his arms. Unfortunately, he became wedged, and it became clearly apparent that he wasn't going to squeeze the rest of his torso through. After using some unsavory language to vent his frustration, he asked Dan to help pull him back out.

"If only I was a bit slimmer!" Robert whined.

"Like me?" Dan retorted slyly.

"I hope you're not insinuating what I think you are," Robert cautioned him with a stern look.

"What other options do you have right now?" Dan challenged him.

"We'll find a sharp rock and..."

"...And you think you can finish the job in what little amount of daylight we have left?"

"Not if we stand around here all day arguing. You don't have the training to attempt a mission like this. For starters, that rope is gonna be ten to thirty feet short of the target. This time of year, the river's quite shallow, so it could be a hard landing."

"And you're a lot heavier than I am," Dan countered.

Robert ignored his observation and quickly continued, "secondly, you need to make contact with someone, without being seen by the wrong people."

Dan could sense from his facial expression, that Robert was starting to warm up to the idea.

"Did you know that as a child, I was undefeated in hide and seek? No lie," Dan boasted as he held up his right hand.

While his playful words suggested he was in good spirits, the truth is he was covering for his true feelings, as usual. Inside, he was extremely anxious over Eve's wellbeing. The fact he kept a somber face throughout, attested to the fact. He was also trying to induce confidence in Robert, who was having second and third doubts about allowing such a venture.

After a brief but intense staring contest, Robert caved, metaphorically speaking of course.

"I can't believe I'm agreeing to this. Talk about your baptism by fire."

Upon hearing this, Dan wasted no time. He quickly grabbed the rope and looped it around his right ankle, just as he had seen Robert do. In no time at all, he had lowered himself through the opening. Robert had given him instructions as he was squeezing into the cave; mainly, not to talk to anyone except for Chief Q or Michael. He then handed Dan's utility belt down to him, followed by his bow and quiver. He wanted Dan to take the gun, but he refused, saying he didn't really know how to use it. He felt he could get more accuracy with his arrows. Robert jokingly asked him if he wanted to wear a cowbell as well, in order to alert any potential foes.

After securing all his gear, Dan looked down at his surroundings. With the sun so low in the sky, very little light was entering through the cave's new opening. The lights below him had a sort of hazing effect. This made it difficult to determine with certainty whether anyone was lurking in the shadows or not. But he knew there were no other options. Slowly but steadily, he lowered himself down until he had reached the end of his rope, literally. Now, he could see his environment much better. There didn't appear to be anyone around. He judged the river to be no more than fifteen feet below, square in the mid-range of Robert's estimate.

He untangled his leg from the rope. Within seconds, he could feel his biceps burning, from carrying the full weight of his body and gear. He took a deep breath and prepared for a landing. As soon as he released the rope, his body was drawn like a magnet to the cool waters below. Knowing that tensing his body would only make the impact more jarring, he relaxed his muscles the best he could. He landed feet first, then briefly keeled over backwards, before standing up. The water came up to his lower ribs. The entry had been as smooth as could be expected. He hoped no one was in earshot of the splashdown, as he scanned the area again. Looking up, he let out a sharp whistle. He knew Robert had heard it, because the rope suddenly started slinking upwards. Dan was glad he didn't have to push his luck and whistle again.

He quickly removed his gear and took off his wet shirt, which was starting to feel very cold and clammy against his skin. After tying it around his waist, he slung the bow and arrows onto his bare back. Drips of water gravitated from his hair, down his torso, and were sucked into the ground beneath him. Realizing that the task which lay ahead was likely his riskiest ever, he felt a sudden surge of adrenalin course through his body.

Up above, Robert was busy covering up the makeshift entrance with a dead log he'd managed to roll onto it. Because any new shafts of light beaming into the cave, were sure to be noticed. Laying down beside it, he nervously awaited the sound of Dan's signal. Each minute that passed only served to heighten his anxiety. Gazing up at the late afternoon sky, he stared at the nearly full moon which was gaining in luminosity. It wouldn't be long now, before the stars began to reveal themselves as well.

Chapter Thirteen

Visiting Hours

There were sounds of someone struggling to fit a key into the hole of the security room door. Inside, Chad spun around in his chair, turning his back on the monitors. Weapon in hand, he took aim at the entrance and waited silently. His trigger finger tensed up as the door slowly swung open.

"Hey, take it easy Chad! You look like a nervous Nellie," Mark spouted. "We already scoured the place for weapons, remember? And we have all the guardian's keys too."

"And can you guarantee me that Robert and Bill are out of the picture for good?"

"Even if one or more of them *did* come around, we'd see 'em coming and deal with it," Mark boasted confidently.

"That might be reassuring...if I didn't have more faith in Robert's abilities than yours," Chad retorted cynically.

Although offended, Mark thought it prudent to keep his mouth shut.

"Any sign of success from the worker bees yet?" Chad inquired.

"Nothing yet."

"I think I need to send out a P.A. announcement, to remind them of their deadline tomorrow evening," added Chad. "And you're sure you scoured the old man's suite from top to bottom?"

"I'm positive. There really wasn't much in there. The only thing I couldn't figure out was the notepad on his desk," Mark revealed casually.

"What notepad?"

"Yeah, it had only a few words written in it, and in some Indian language."

"And you didn't think it might be worth looking into?" Chad asked with an air of exasperation in his voice.

"Well why would he leave it out in the open like that? And who here would understand it anyway?" Mark reasoned.

"That's exactly why he would just leave it out in the open!" Chad raised his voice, before calming himself down. "First, go get the notepad. Then, go over to the library. Get any books on native languages you can find, and bring it all back here."

"You got it," Mark said obediently.

"Oh, and try not to stumble over your own feet while doing all that," Chad threw in contemptuously.

Mark had some choice words for Chad, but he only dared to mumble them under his breath, as he closed the door on his way out.

It seemed eerily quiet, as Dan made his way through the living quarters. What he couldn't have known was that everyone was trying to get some rest. Although it wouldn't be easy to fall asleep, under the circumstances. They were all dead tired from frantically searching for Chad's treasure. Early in the morning they would all be back at it, as the deadline loomed ever closer.

Dan was walking along the tier which led to Chief Q's abode, scanning far ahead and constantly checking over his shoulder. Normally, there would be neighbors chatting with one another here and there. The absence of normal social activity made Dan uncomfortable. About forty feet from his destination, he heard a door suddenly open behind him, immediately increasing his heart-rate.

"Dan," a female voice called out to him in a hushed manner, as he turned around to see who it was.

"Oh hi, it's Susan, right?"

"Yes. Quick, get inside."

As Dan entered, she quickly poked her head out to the right, before closing and locking the door.

"What's happened here since we left?" Dan wondered anxiously.

"Come to the back of the room here first, away from the door," Susan gestured.

Dan followed her lead.

"I'm so glad you're alive and well," she said as she embraced him. "How are Bill and Robert?"

"They're fine too. And we brought my mother back with us."

"That's great. Where are they now?" she asked with concern.

"They're all on the outside. I'm here alone to gather info on the situation."

"Well, I'm glad to hear they're okay. And I'm glad they're not here with you."

"So, *what is* going on?" he asked impatiently.

"Chad let in three of his thug friends and took over Eos," Susan replied bluntly.

"Chad?" Dan said in disbelief. "Why would he do something like that?"

"He thinks Katzman might have hid a fortune in here before he passed away. It's always about the money," she added cynically. "Anyway, he tampered with your vehicles before you guys left."

"Where is he now?" Dan asked.

"I'm not sure, but I saw one of his henchmen going into Chief Q's place just moments before you came along."

Dan now understood her behaviour.

"Boy, it's a good thing you saw me when you did then. I was just headed over there myself."

"And you would have been wasting your time," Susan stated, as a sullen look suddenly came over her face.

"What do you mean?"

"They killed Chief Q," she stated robotically.

"What?" Dan asked in total disbelief.

The two then stared silently at each other, as the reality of it sunk in.

"What about the others? Is everyone else okay?"

The lack of an immediate response from Susan, and the look in her eyes, almost made Dan's heart stop. Without even mentioning her name, they both knew it was Eve that they were thinking about.

"Look Dan, I'm not going to lie to you. She's in pretty bad shape. She's been in a coma since yesterday."

"Where is she?!"

"Ssssh!" Susan said, as she put her index finger over her mouth. "She's in the clinic. We've been taking turns monitoring her condition."

"What happened to her?" Dan asked in a less audible tone this time.

"Chad was bragging about how he sabotaged you guys. Then he said even if any of you made it back, they'd be ready for you. That set her off like a stick of dynamite, and she attacked him. Then Chad hit her in the head hard, with his gun."

"I have to see her," Dan announced impetuously.

"No. That's too risky," Susan objected. We know that one of them is in the security room, and another is at the entrance. But the other two could be anywhere."

"I'm sorry, but I have to see her. I'll be very careful," Dan assured her.

"Then let me help you. I'll make sure it's all clear."

"Thanks for the offer, but I don't want to put you in any danger."

"You won't be. My presence there would seem perfectly innocent to them."

"Alright," Dan conceded, "let's go."

Susan led him to the door, opened it, and looked both ways.

"It's all clear. I noticed someone walking outside a few moments ago, behind you. It was probably that guy, coming back from Chief Q's place. Keep looking behind you in case it wasn't, and try to keep me in sight," Susan advised him, as she headed toward the clinic.

Having safely made their way there, Susan waited for Dan at the door, before leading him inside. Her husband Jack was reading a book at Eve's bedside. When he saw Dan, entering behind his wife, his eyes lit up and he stood. Susan immediately put her hand over his mouth and cautioned him.

"Don't talk too loud, we don't want to attract any unsavory characters."

"Okay," he replied softly, as he put his book down before greeting Dan with a handshake.

Of course, he was eager to hear all about Dan's expedition. But even as Dan was talking to him, Jack could see that his eyes were fixated on Eve. Susan pulled her husband away, saying she would explain everything outside. Dan slowly walked over to the bed as the door closed behind him. As he stood over Eve, he noticed how peaceful she appeared. It was as if she had just laid down for a little nap. The IV drip and the heart monitor looked strangely out of place, against the rustic backdrop of wood and stone.

"I don't know if you can hear me, but I'll do all the talking if you don't mind," he quipped with a poker face.

He gently lifted her left hand and caressed it.

"I can't believe you pulled that stunt with Chad. I guess that's just who you are. Personally, I'm still trying to figure out who *I* am."

Dan laid her hand back down and reached into his pants pocket. He fished out a damp five-dollar note and stretched it out flat. He then inserted it into Eve's limp hand while giving her instructions.

"I want to see you spending this real soon."

After kissing her forehead, he ran the back of his hand down her cheek. He had momentarily forgotten about the situation at hand. Reality quickly set back in, and he turned to leave. He nervously cracked the door open and poked his head out. Jack and Susan had been vigilantly surveying the area.

"All clear," Susan said quietly, as she gave Dan the two thumbs up sign. "What's your next move?"

"I have to get back to the river and let Robert know what's going on," Dan replied.

"Well I hope he comes up with a plan. And really quick too."

"Why do you say that?" Dan wondered.

"Because they're planning to kill one of us every forty-eight hours until we find their treasure."

"What? That's crazy," Dan said as he shook his head in disgust. "How much time do we have left?"

"Until six o'clock tomorrow evening," Susan answered.

"Don't worry. We won't let that happen," Dan stated defiantly.

***

Mark placed a stack of six books on the counter in front of Chad, who picked up the smaller one on top.

"Is this the notebook?" he asked.

"Yup, that's the one," Mark replied.

Chad picked it up and glanced at the first page. There were eight words written on it, in single file from top to bottom. He quickly put the open notebook aside and went on to the next book. They were all dictionaries of Southwestern native languages.

When he compared Chief Q's words with the fourth dictionary, he realized he'd found a match. The words used were in Navajo. After excitedly translating the first three words, he realized they were seemingly random. But he continued, hoping the complete text would somehow make sense. After reading the words aloud however, Chad was sorely disappointed.

"This is nothing but incoherent gibberish! It's probably some stupid Indian prayer or something!"

He furiously slid the books onto the floor, with one violent swoop.

Out of curiosity, Mark picked up the notebook and looked at the translations.

"Fox, ice, snake, horse...these are mostly just animals," he declared.

"Well at least now I know you're not illiterate!" Chad vented. "*What would* I do without you?"

He grabbed the microphone and pressed the button at the base of the stand.

"*Attention all residents...!*" He barked.

When Dan heard the P.A. system come on, it made him jump in his tracks, as he walked through the corridor leading to the small cavern. Chad's sudden outburst gave his heart a jumpstart it didn't need, seeing as he was already on edge.

"*...This is a friendly reminder of tomorrow's six o'clock deadline, if you'll pardon the play on words. At that time, one of you will be sacrificed for the cause. Unless you can deliver the goods by then, of course. So, I suggest you all get a good night's sleep and start again tomorrow, bright and early!*"

Chad's public rant was really nothing more than a power trip of course. In reality, no one needed any reminding, or encouragement. Most of them wouldn't even be able to sleep, under the circumstances. Some were trying to rest or get some nourishment, others were gathering to exchange ideas and draw up search plans. Just before Dan's arrival, the caves had been abuzz with activity. Everyone had been giving their all toward the effort.

As Dan reached the riverbank, he took a spinning glance around. As quickly as he could, he pulled the notebook out of the backpack and began writing away. After listing all the main news items, Dan informed Robert of his plans, and expeditiously inserted the notebook back into the bag. Deciding it was safe to do so, he aimed a high-pitched whistle upwards, toward Robert.

Within seconds, a para-cord with a fist sized rock began dropping from the ceiling. About thirty feet from the water it suddenly stopped, and began swinging from side to side like a pendulum. After gaining momentum, it was now spanning beyond the width of the narrow river. The large stone suddenly shot over to Dan's side of the water and landed in some rocks. He quickly retrieved it, untied the stone, and replaced it with his backpack. Two more firm tugs alerted his companion to hoist it up.

Up top, Robert reeled the rope in with a sense of urgency. He felt like a fisherman, when he feels a bite. With nervous anxiety, he birthed the bag from the opening. While waiting for Dan to complete his mission, he had felt a sense of complete helplessness. It wasn't an easy task, for someone who likes to feel like he's in control of every situation. A few lines into the message, he could tell that his worst fears had come to pass. The last part of Dan's report he would normally have found unacceptable. But under the circumstances, he really couldn't argue against it

"*Time is short. Since I'm safely here, decided to stay and try to resolve situation. Take care of my mother. Will meet u outside entrance tomorrow nineteen hundred. If I'm not there, you'll have to come up with plan B. know u won't like this, but can't risk Eve's life, or others.*"

Indeed, Robert didn't like it one bit. He also knew he wouldn't be able to change Dan's mind. Even if he could, it would mean pulling him back up and then descending again tomorrow, with all the risks that entailed. Reluctantly, he quickly jotted down his positive response and returned the notebook to the backpack, along with his handgun. He knew very well how Dan felt about guns, but figured he wouldn't want to press his luck; common sense dictated that it wouldn't be prudent to play ping-pong with the backpack. Although this area would be considered low priority, eventually someone would come along to patrol it.

After it came back into his possession, Dan opened the bag and quickly devoured Robert's short response.

"*I understand. Find a safe place for the night. Suggest farming enclosure. Hide gun in your sock. Use thick rubber band to secure. Try to find Michael. Use extreme caution. May God be with you. See you tomorrow night.*"

Chapter Fourteen

Declaration of War

Some of the residents awoke to the smell of coffee, others to an alarm. In Dan's case, the first thing his senses were greeted with, was the lick of a lamb on his cheek. Not being something one would normally awaken to, it was rather startling. As soon as his eyes opened, he found himself face to face with his woolly new friend. After a couple of seconds, he remembered where he was. Farmer Willie had wanted Dan to bunk down in his quarters, but it would have been a little risky. So here he was, lying on a makeshift mattress of hay bales. As he scratched the lamb's neck, Dan heard Willie calling out from behind the wall of hay in front of him.

"Mornin' city slicker! Up and at 'em!"

When he came into view, Dan could see he was holding a plate of breakfast.

"I hope you like bacon and eggs."

"Good morning," Dan said as he combed his hair with his fingers. "I *love* bacon and eggs."

He didn't know which smelled better, the bacon or the pan-fried potatoes. This was his first real meal since the grilled grouse almost twenty-four hours earlier.

"Thank you so much," Dan said sincerely.

"Don't mention it. I just carried it from the cafeteria. I didn't actually prepare it or nuthin'."

As Dan dove right into the pile of hash-browns, Willie sat down across from him and pulled the lamb toward himself, away from Dan's plate.

"So, what's your next move?" he asked Dan.

"I guess I should try and contact Michael first. Any idea where I might find him?"

"He's normally wandering all over the place as it is, now with this treasure hunt going on, he could be anywhere."

"That's what I figured," Dan said between bites.

"Is there anything I can do to help you?" Willie offered.

"I appreciate you asking, but with your skills and knowledge, you're not as dispensable as I am," Dan answered frankly.

"You're a very brave and unusually responsible young man," Willie praised him.

Dan graciously smiled as he accepted the flattering compliment. The farmer's kind words had a bigger impact on him than Willie could possibly have known, just by Dan's expression. The truth is they helped fill a void deep down in Dan's subconscious. The only praises that Dan could remember had been few, and far between. And even then, they were always for some athletic achievement, never for any redeeming character traits.

"Well if you change your mind, you know where to find me," Willie said, as he stood up. "If you'll excuse me, I have to get back to my animals now. They're almost as hungry as you are."

"Of course, thanks for everything," Dan replied, as he stuck his fork into a slice of bacon.

***

The band of teens, two boys and two girls, roamed the apartment hallways, trying each doorknob along the way. When they found one unlocked, they entered cautiously.

"Hello!" Anybody home?" the taller male called out, just inside the doorway.

The lack of a response emboldened them, as they locked the door behind them. After doing a quick scan of the premises, the taller one, the leader apparently, headed for the living room window. He opened the blinds completely, to allow in as much light as possible. It was a clear afternoon, and the nearly direct sunlight invaded the suite. As per their plan, they all spread out and began searching for any food they could find.

"Ew, the fruit in this bowl is all moldy," whined Suzy, the younger, red-haired girl.

"Jackpot!" rejoiced her older brother Tyler, as he returned from the kitchen.

He was clutching a bag of chips in one hand, and a big bottle of cola in the other.

"I saw some nuts and candy bars in there too!" he added, sending the others off on a mad dash into the kitchen.

As they made themselves at home on the large, cream-colored sofa, they feasted on their loot.

"I think we should crash here for a while," declared the tall, blond-haired male. "This place is cool, and there's a butt-load of snacks in the pantry, even if most of it is weird health food stuff."

"You think it's safe?" asked the skinny girl, the older of the two.

"Sure, look around...whoever lived here must have planned for a long trip," replied her boyfriend. "And I'm pretty sure we're not the first visitors since then, by the looks of it."

Claire, the thin brunette, walked over to the large aquarium and peered inside, unsurprisingly, the once crystalline water had become quite murky. She opened the lid and tossed in a few pinches of the flakes.

"Why bother?" Suzy queried, "They'll all be dead soon anyway."

"Too bad there's no way to cook them," teased her boyfriend, as the other two laughed.

"Oh, you're so mean," replied Claire.

After closing the lid, she perused the various maintenance items underneath the aquarium stand. She was particularly interested in the book titled, 'Keeping a happy saltwater aquarium.' She sat down in the loveseat by the sofa, and continued reading.

"Oh, here we go again," complained her boyfriend. "Claire the undercover vet, is on the case."

"You know," she proclaimed, "I think I can keep them alive, at least until the nights get too cold. This explains how to maintain the proper salinity levels and everything."

"You don't even have any water," Suzy reminded her.

"Yes we do," she claimed. "I saw big jugs of bottled water in the kitchen, behind the water cooler."

"So, you're gonna waste it on the fish?" protested her boyfriend.

"You only drink soda anyway. What do you care?" Claire retorted with disdain.

"Don't you need *seawater*?" inquired Suzy.

"No. They've got water purifier there, and special salt and everything," Claire pointed out.

As she began to remove some of the turbid tank-water with an empty pail she had found, Claire suddenly had a lightbulb moment.

"You know what?" she exclaimed excitedly, "We can use this water to flush the toilet!"

"Way to recycle!" cheered Suzy, "And, we can start collecting rainwater on the balcony too," she added.

The two boys were visibly impressed, and at the same time, wished they'd thought of it. Claire's boyfriend managed to redeem his gender a few moments later, with an idea of his own.

"I've got it! I know how we can keep ourselves warm at night, and maybe keep your fish alive through the Autumn," he claimed proudly.

"This I gotta hear," Suzy said cynically.

"I can set up a woodstove in here using a steel drum!"

"Tell me you're not serious," begged Tyler.

"No, seriously! I can use sheet metal to form an exhaust duct out to the balcony. I can cut an opening in the glass, and then seal it. We're on the top floor anyway. The smoke shouldn't bother any neighbors, if we even have any still. And I know just where to get the welding torch, glass cutter and everything else I need, all in one stop."

"And that would be where exactly?" asked Claire.

"At the high school," he responded.

"You're going to break into the school?" Claire questioned him.

"I probably wouldn't have to," he claimed. "For sure most of the windows are broken by now, by people looking for food and stuff. But I'll bet the metal shop still has what I need, as well as the woodworking class. I'll also need to find some bricks or rocks somewhere, for the base."

If Claire was the vet of the group, then her boyfriend Tom, was the handyman. Despite his horrendous academic grades, he had aced his metalwork and woodworking classes.

"Well, if you insist on going down there, take Tyler with you, and be really careful. You'll probably encounter other people there, scrounging around," Claire worried.

"You mean criminals like us?" suggested Suzy.

"We're not criminals, we didn't break in here," protested Tyler. "The door was open. Right Tom?"

"That's right," he agreed, "and we're not stealing anything. We're just borrowing things for a while."

"So, we're just *borrowing* these chips?" Suzy laughed, as she munched.

As her three accomplices debated the ethics of their activities, Claire went into the kitchen to retrieve some fresh water.

***

He was a tall, slender young man, clean shaven and with short brown hair. In short, he looked like the stereotypical medical student. His parents had wanted him to become a doctor. A worthy profession, one which allows you to help mankind, and make a comfortable living for yourself at the same time. They had worked hard to send him to medical school. Unfortunately, he just didn't have the aptitude for medicine, failing miserably in his first year. Now, here he was, three years later. Ironically, finding himself involved in an endeavor which had claimed at least one life, so far.

As he walked to the clinic early, on what appeared to be another brilliant morning outside, he couldn't help but wonder what his parents would think of him now. As he stopped and knocked on the clinic door, a shaft of light was illuminating him from behind. It gave him an angelic appearance which was most unfitting. Indeed, when Susan opened the door, it didn't prevent the look of disgust which immediately came upon her face.

"Oh...you must be the *fourth* stooge."

"Susan! Settle down. There's been more than enough trouble already," Doctor Monroe interjected.

"That's okay, I deserve it," the visitor stated calmly. "Actually, my name is Ryan."

He offered his right hand out to greet Susan, but she only glared at it with contempt. After lowering his hand awkwardly, he asked if he could enter.

"If you have to," Susan replied as she stepped to the side, allowing him access.

"I just wanted to see how the girl was doing," he said, slowly approaching Eve.

"Your guess is as good as ours. All I can tell you is that her vital signs are stable," Susan proclaimed disdainfully. "And since when did you start caring?"

"I can imagine what you must think of me, but I really didn't mean to bring harm to anyone. I thought we were just stealing from the rich to give to the poor...you know? I mean, here's Katzman, with his mountains of money, which he probably didn't even have to sweat for. Then the rest of us have to strive so hard and hustle our sorry asses just to pay the bills."

Susan just stood by, with arms crossed, nodding her head slowly from side to side.

"You keep telling yourself that, if it makes you feel justified."

Ryan had no response to that. After all, it sounded just as lame to *his* ears. And he was the one saying it. Instead, he changed the subject and pointed to the five-dollar bill in Eve's hand.

"What's with the money?"

Without missing a beat, the doctor suddenly jumped into the conversation.

"Oh, that's my lucky money. It's the first five dollars I ever made, selling lemonade when I was nine years old."

Susan was impressed, and a little relieved. She was frantically trying to come up with some story herself. Suddenly, as if on cue, Eve's foot twitched quite noticeably. As the three of them fixed their gaze on her, Eve's eyes pried themselves open and then fluttered. Without moving her head, she weakly raised her right hand at the elbow, until she could see what she was holding. Having satisfied her curiosity, she then cracked a labored grin, put her head back down and closed her eyes.

"Boy, you weren't kidding Doc. That fiver really is lucky," Ryan stated only half jokingly.

Susan and Doctor Monroe looked at each other with joy and relief. Joy that Eve seemed to be coming out of the coma, and relief that she hadn't spoken, and given them away.

"I assume that's a good sign?" Ryan asked.

"*Very* good," answered the Doctor.

"I can't tell you how happy I am to hear that," continued Ryan.

Susan stared at him with confusion and wonderment before speaking.

"If you're such a humanitarian, how can you just blindly follow Chad, regardless of the consequences?" she challenged.

"Like I said, I had no idea anyone was going to lose their life over this," Ryan claimed in his own defence.

"What about his plan to systematically murder us one by one? You haven't seen that coming yet either?" Susan pushed back.

"Actually, I have an alternative that I'm going to propose to Chad. I think I know a way for us to avoid anymore bloodshed."

"And what if he doesn't accept your proposal?" She inquired.

Ryan lowered his eyes and just stood there silently. He honestly didn't know what his reaction would be.

"That's what I thought," Susan declared judgementally, before walking over to the door and opening it wide. "I'm sorry. Visiting hours are over," she announced coldly, with her hand still on the doorknob.

Without any further word, Ryan exited the clinic looking rather dejected. Any sympathy he hoped to have earned never materialized. He really didn't want to see anyone else getting hurt. At the same time, this was too good an opportunity to pass up, and he was now deeply entrenched in it. He was left sitting firmly on the fence, and the grass looked equally as green on either side.

Arriving at the security room, Ryan was glad to find Chad there, staring pensively at the surveillance monitors. Chad took a quick glance to his left to see who had entered.

"I guess the guardians are out of the picture. There's been no sign of them yet," Chad informed Ryan, who pulled up a chair next to him.

"Say, I've been thinking. Maybe there's a way we can do this thing with no more bloodshed," Ryan stated confidently.

"Oh? And just how would that work?" Chad asked curiously.

"How about if we just pretend like we offed one of them today, but just lock them up in here instead?"

"And you don't think it'll look suspicious, when all these dead bodies begin to pile up, with no corpses to be found? Or if this room begins to fill up with them, and we have to cart in loads of extra food everyday? You seem to forget that these are some highly intelligent people we're dealing with here. When they figure out it's just a game, they'll wait till we've 'killed' them all and left, and they win. And if they did happen to find the loot, they would just keep it under wraps. There would be no reason for them to hand it over to us."

Ryan was visibly disappointed to hear all this.

"What's the matter? Are you getting cold feet?" Chad challenged him.

"No. I just don't understand why we have to kill people to pull this off, that's all."

"Well, if our friend Mark hadn't popped the Chief, we might not have had to go down this road," Chad pointed out as he tried to deflect the blame.

Ryan wasn't about to let him off so easily though.

"What about that hermit you killed?"

"That guy was mentally unstable and very nosy. That's a dangerous combination. Heck, I probably did him a favor. What kind of life is that? Foraging around in the wilderness like an animal. I'll tell you what; I'm willing to compromise with you. If we don't have any success after a week, then we'll use your method. I figure if no one finds anything by then, they probably never will."

"Then what?" Ryan wondered.

"Then we leave. It's not like they're going to ask for help from the outside. Meanwhile, we recruit a few more partners and get some heavy-duty treasure hunting toys; metal detectors, scanners, etcetera. When we have enough personnel, we come back and put everyone under house arrest. Then we can do the job right, ourselves. The four of us can't keep hundreds of people at bay indefinitely. Sooner or later, they'll hatch a plan to revolt."

"And you're convinced Katzman hid a fortune in this place?" Ryan asked, seeking affirmation.

"It's the only thing that makes sense," Chad asserted. "How could they bring all these people out here with no contingency? After six months, they'd start getting sick and dying off. Also, do you recall the Chief denying it before he died?"

"What if he was the only one who knew about it?" Ryan added.

"Again, there are some real geniuses here and they've put a lot of time and labor into Eos. I can't believe they wouldn't think of all the possibilities and plan accordingly."

Ryan had no arguments left, and just stared aimlessly into a monitor.

"You sure you're not getting cold feet?" Chad asked suspiciously. "Because if you are, you're free to leave anytime. That's one more share of the spoils for the rest of us."

Ryan knew very well that Chad wasn't about to let anyone just walk away from Eos. This was just a test.

"No, I'm in too deep now. As far as the law is concerned, I'm an accessory to murder. I was just putting another option out there."

"Well, if you have any more brainstorms, don't be afraid to share. I'm all ears," Chad stated slyly.

"Yeah, I will," Ryan replied as he stood up to leave. I'll see you later. I better get back to my patrol."

"Don't be a stranger," Chad called out as the door closed.

Tapping a pen on the counter, he stared at the door pensively. Suspicions about Ryan's loyalty, or rather lack thereof, had begun to emerge.

***

"It's no use," Michael lamented to Ranjit. "It's like looking for a needle in a haystack,"

The two of them were both peering through binoculars, scouring the upper walls of the main cave. What they hoped to find was some anomaly in the cracks and crevices; anything that appeared artificial or unnatural in color, shape, or texture.

"I pray someone is having better fortunes elsewhere my friend," hoped Ranjit.

The harsh reality was that no one was, and time was not on their side. They were now minutes away from the six o'clock deadline.

Pretty much everyone in the facility was scrambling to locate any evidence of a financial stash. But amidst the desperation, a handful of residents were taking a different approach. One of these was Father James. He was in the prayer room, along with Rabbi Yosef and the imam. The trio of prayer warriors had given up the search a couple of hours earlier. Somehow, without consulting one another, they had all gravitated to the same conclusion and to the same physical place. When the door behind them opened, they all turned curiously to see who was about to join them. It was Ryan. Their assumption of course, was that he was there to collect one of them for the first sacrifice.

"Sorry to interrupt, I was wondering if I could talk to Father James privately."

When the priest stood up, the other two began to rise as well.

"It's all right," he reassured them. "Please...continue."

They reluctantly agreed and sat back down, as he slipped his rosary into his jacket pocket and walked outside with Ryan. After closing the door, Father James immediately initiated the conversation.

"What can I help you with?"

"I was wondering if you'd be able to hear my confession," Ryan replied rather meekly.

"What? You're a Catholic?"

"Kind of," said Ryan.

The priest's first thought was to reprimand him, and then to point out the theological error of his last statement. However, he was wise enough to realize that it would be the wrong approach. He had to reach deep down, in order to muster the restraint and compassion needed to react calmly.

"Yes, I could. But you must realize, I can't give you absolution. That would require not only your repentance, but your willingness to carry out the penance. Normally, I would ask that you turn yourself over to the authorities. In this case however, that would compromise this whole operation. I can tell you right now what your penance would include; trying to prevent any further crimes, removing yourself from Eos, and trying to make restitution. Is that something you'd be able to agree to?"

"I...I really don't know," Ryan stuttered.

"Look, you obviously feel some sense of guilt, or you wouldn't be here right now. I suggest you contemplate a certain scriptural verse. The one that says, '...For what shall it profit a man if he gains the whole world but loses his soul.'"

And with that, Father James turned and slipped back into the quiet room, leaving Ryan to mull over his situation.

At precisely six o'clock Chad made a P.A. announcement. He informed his listeners that since no one had stepped forward with any discovery, he would have to carry out his threat. Ironically, the garden in the center of the secondary cavern was his chosen locale for the public execution. Although everyone wondered who his selected victim would be, Chad made no mention of the identity. And despite their curiosity, almost everyone had decided not to attend. They wanted to neither witness the grisly act, nor give the culprits any satisfaction.

A few of the men had been discussing a revolt. They wanted to overcome the intruders with their superior numbers. It had been the religious leaders who had urged them not to. They pointed out that despite the odds being in their favor, it could result in untold carnage. Father James had asked them to allow him to try and resolve the situation peacefully first. If he wasn't successful, they could always resort to a more hands-on approach later.

Father James was the first person, besides Chad, to arrive at the garden. They were soon joined by Ryan, who accompanied an older male resident at gunpoint. The priest had seen this man in the cafeteria a few times, but had yet to meet his acquaintance. He gave a compassionate nod of the head to him, before offering an icy stare to Ryan, who immediately looked away in shame. The selected victim was a chemist. His role was mainly as an advisor to the other caretakers, as he didn't have any specific duties, per say.

He and Ryan stopped a few feet from Chad, who was resting his left leg on a park bench. Without saying a word, he walked right up to the man and stuck his gun square into the middle of his chest.

"I'll make this as quick as possible for you," Chad told him coldly.

"Wait!" Father James called out. "I'd like to take his place."

Chad was rather surprised by the priest's request, and seemed to consider it, for a brief moment.

"Why, that's mighty brave of you Padre. Unfortunately, I can't agree to that. People might think this works on a volunteer basis, and they might get too comfortable. Knowing that any one of them could be next will keep them honest."

Father James looked over to Ryan with a stern countenance. Ryan made eye contact with him momentarily, before looking away despondently. The exchange didn't go unnoticed by Chad. He glared at Father James with a cynical grin, as if to claim some sort of psychological victory. Ryan cringed and turned away as Chad put his finger on the trigger.

Suddenly, the monastic silence of the cavern was violently interrupted by the cracking sound of gunfire, with an echo that lingered. The single shot was fired from a few hundred feet away. It had come from behind the banana plants in the tropical garden. To say that the four men were startled would be a gross understatement. A suddenly panic stricken Chad quickly scanned the lush vegetation to his right.

"Where did that come from?!" he yelled to Ryan, after failing to spot anyone.

"I think somebody's hiding in the garden over there," he responded.

"Let's get out of here! And watch your back!" Chad hollered, as he half-turned and ran toward the corridor.

To Father James, the two men looked like rats scurrying away, after having had their lair disturbed.

Chapter Fifteen

Redemption

From behind the banana leaves, a head popped out. It was Michael, holding Robert's gun.

"It worked. They're gone," he said to Dan, who was right beside him holding his bow.

He'd had the good fortune of spotting Michael, treasure hunting with Ranjit.

"I'm glad Robert insisted on giving me that gun. I don't think an arrow would've had quite the same effect," Dan had to admit.

"Unfortunately, we've used up our element of surprise," said Michael. "We know one of them is at the entrance and one will be in the security room. As for the other two, they could be anywhere."

"I figure they must be headed to the security room," Dan reasoned. "They'll be wondering if someone came in through the entrance."

"Good point," Michael concurred.

"While they're busy in there, we need to get the guy at the entrance and let Robert in," Dan suggested.

"Sounds like a plan. Let's go!" Michael urged, as he began jogging in that direction.

Indeed, Chad and Ryan had fled to the security room. Their entry was so abrupt and violent, that Mark spilled half his coffee onto himself.

"What the hell!" he complained, as he stood up and looked at his shirt and pants.

Chad couldn't have cared less about Mark's little calamity.

"Have you been watching those monitors the whole time?" Chad demanded to know.

"Yeah...why?" Mark asked.

"Someone fired off a gun at us just now!"

"I thought you said the only people with guns in this place were guardians," Mark shot back. "And we went through their quarters with a fine-tooth comb. The only other weapons are in this room, and *we* control it."

"Maybe one of the other residents smuggled it in when they came here," Ryan figured.

"That's possible, but unlikely. That would go against the character of a chosen one. They were carefully screened, remember?" Chad reminded him.

"Then what's your theory?" Mark challenged him.

"What if there's another way in here besides the front entrance? What if Robert and Bill knew about it? And what if one or more of them came back in here? They know where all the cameras are. That would explain how we didn't notice anything unusual," Chad concluded.

"Either way, our job just got a lot more dangerous," said Mark. "What are we supposed to do now?"

"For starters, you can shut up and let me think!" Chad bellowed.

He sat down at the monitoring table and ran his hands through his hair. Staring into the main screen covering the entrance, he tried to brainstorm his next move.

"Shit!" he suddenly cried out, instantly grabbing the attention of his two associates.

"What is it?" asked Ryan.

Chad stood and pointed at the screen.

"Look!"

What they all saw was Ian, their fourth partner in crime, being disarmed by Michael and Dan. They had taken advantage of a window of opportunity. Ian had sat down and laid his weapon beside him. As he gnawed on a strip of beef jerky, Dan and Michael suddenly popped up at the foot of the stairs, with gun and bow drawn. In the security room, they could see Ian with his arms raised, as the two slowly crept up the steps.

With Michael covering him, Dan put his bow behind him and picked up Ian's rifle. He then unlocked the front doors, swung one open, and went outside. As Chad and company watched in disgust, they could see him making his way around the house to the front gate. Upon reaching it, he used his access card to open it. They weren't very surprised to see Robert come running up to Dan. Not seeing Bill with them, chad assumed he hadn't survived the trip.

"There's three of them altogether, and they have two guns, thanks to that rocket scientist Ian!"

"Should we go get 'em?" Mark offered.

"No, they won't be dumb enough to stay in our lines of sight. At some point or other, they'll end up coming here," Chad opined.

"And we'll be ready for 'em," Mark figured.

"No," said Chad, surprisingly. "You keep forgetting that they're not as stupid as you. They would just hold us hostage in here till we either surrendered, or died of dehydration."

Although he agreed with Chad's assessment, Mark wished he'd stop questioning his intelligence...and his face showed the resentment.

"So, what do we do then?" Ryan wondered.

"Help me grab the weapons out of the armory, then follow me!" Chad ordered.

After doing so, they ran out of the room with three or four rifles apiece, slung over their shoulders.

A few minutes later, the guardians arrived at the security room. Robert and Dan got there first. Michael and his handcuffed prisoner arrived from a different direction. They had split up, so as not to become easy targets for a sniper attack.

Oddly enough, they found that the door to the security room had been left wide open.

"They've either given up and left, or it's an ambush," Michael suggested.

From about a hundred yards away, Robert could see most of the monitoring station, but little else. He got Dan to babysit Ian, while he and Michael cautiously approached from opposing angles. As they closed in, each one could see more and more of the interior. It all seemed clear. Just as they had planned ahead of time, Michael waited for Robert's signal. When he gave Michael a full nod of the head, they both dropped down on all fours and dove into the room. Together, they had both sides of the doorway covered with their guns. The room was indeed empty. They quickly picked themselves up off the floor. Michael stepped outside and called out to Dan.

"All clear!"

Dan looked around nervously, as he nudged Ian toward the room. Inside, Robert and Michael began snooping around. Robert noticed that the armory had been emptied. Both doors had been flung wide open. A piece of paper had been taped to the inside of the left door. As Michael quickly sifted through the library books on the counter, he noticed Robert pull the page down.

"What does it say?"

Robert proceeded to read out the short letter, as the other two entered the room.

"We're all in the clinic. The three of you need to meet us there and surrender your weapons. If you try to pull any stunts, sleeping beauty will never awaken."

It was meant to be a cryptic message for Michael, but Robert had already been briefed by Dan along the way. He, of course had firsthand knowledge himself, unbeknownst to Chad. The three were all well aware of who 'sleeping beauty' was.

"What are we going to do now?" Dan asked with a most worrisome look.

Robert and Michael could only stare at him in helpless silence.

***

"Here they come!" Mark heralded at the clinic doorway.

In the distance, he could see Michael and the two guardians approaching. Ian had been handcuffed to a water pipe in the security room. The three all carried their weapons slung over their backs.

"When they get about fifty feet away, tell them to put down all their weapons and keep walking. When they get close enough, mow 'em all down," Chad commanded.

Ryan looked at him in disbelief.

"We don't have any prison cells here, and I don't need the extra headaches. Look how much trouble they've caused already," Chad said in response to Ryan's silent protest. "Look on the bright side," he continued, "We'll have filled our quota for the next three days."

Ryan thought back to his earlier conversation with Father James. The priest's words had been nagging at him ever since. Though he didn't dare tell Chad, he had felt tremendous relief when the earlier execution had been interrupted.

"Put your weapons down and walk this way!" Mark ordered the oncoming trio.

As he raised his rifle into shooting position, Ryan made a move which surprised everyone, including himself. He shot his colleague Mark in the left side of the torso, and he collapsed, hitting the hard ground like a sack of potatoes. Chad couldn't believe his eyes, but he instinctively aimed his own rifle at Ryan. Unfortunately for him, another pair of hands pulled the weapon from it's target. It was Eve. She had been conscious the whole time, and was just playing possum. Though Eve was physically no match for Chad, she *was* able to struggle with him, just long enough to allow Ryan to intervene.

"Drop it, or you're next!" he warned forcefully.

With Mark laying in the doorway bleeding to death, Chad wasn't about to doubt Ryan's resolve. He reluctantly released his grip on the gun and raised his hands, as Eve reclined with the rifle. She held it like a child holds a security blanket or stuffed animal. The exertion had given her a headache, and so she closed her eyes to relieve the tension.

Ryan gestured toward the entrance with his rifle.

"Go outside! Move it!" he ordered his former boss.

As they stepped outside, they could see Robert approaching, while the other two went back for the weapons. Ryan knelt on one knee as he put his fingers to Mark's neck, checking for a pulse. Chad figured this would probably be his one chance at escape. Rather than making a grab for Ryan's gun, with the attendant risk of Robert intervening, he decided to flee. If he wasn't grossly misjudging Ryan, he probably wouldn't shoot an unarmed man in the back.

"Stop!" Ryan yelled out, to no avail.

As Chad sprinted away wildly down the path, he suddenly felt a searing pain in the back of his lower leg. It was a complete surprise to him, because what he had been fearing was the sound of gunfire, and there hadn't been any. He had no choice but to stop dead in his tracks. As he looked at his leg in agony, he could see an arrow embedded right into his left calf. His attempted escape was over. All he could do now was sit down on the ground and squeeze the area around the shaft. The pain was excruciating, but there was no way he'd be able to remove the projectile.

"Nice shot!" Robert celebrated. "You just added a turkey to your tally. No wonder you don't need a firearm."

The normally modest Dan had a somewhat proud grin on his face, as he relished the compliment. He didn't have the luxury of wallowing in his glory too long though. He had far more pressing concerns on his mind.

Although they had only heard the one shot, Dan was still concerned for Eve's wellbeing. He strode quickly and purposefully in her direction.

"What just happened in there?" Robert asked Ryan, as he doublechecked Mark for any sign of life.

"He was about to shoot the three of you...so I shot him first," Ryan explained nervously. "I didn't mean to kill him."

"Under the circumstances, I think we can find it in our hearts to forgive you," Robert assured him sarcastically. "But how did you manage to keep Chad at bay?"

"Oh, the girl helped me out with that," Ryan disclosed.

Dan overheard him as he was about to enter the room, and his heart skipped a beat with excitement.

"Augh!" was about the only thing Chad could express, as he writhed in pain.

"Pardon my ignorance, but what made you turn on your own kind like that?" Robert obviously couldn't help but wonder.

"It's a long story actually..." responded Ryan.

"Well, maybe you can fill me in, as we get Chad some medical attention."

The two walked over to Chad and helped him to his feet. They then supported him under each arm as they passed Mark, laying in a pool of blood.

Inside, Eve slowly opened her eyes when she heard Dan's footsteps. It would be a tough call to say who smiled first, such was the synchronicity of their timing.

"You have no idea how glad I am to see you awake," Dan stated with relief.

"As glad as I was to see that money in my hand, maybe?" Eve retorted.

"Boy, you really are materialistic, aren't you?" he joked, sparking unanimous laughter.

"If you don't mind, could you take this heavy thing off my hands?" she requested.

"Of course," Dan said as he took the weapon. "Do these things have some kind of safety lock?" he wondered, as he fumbled around with it. "Never mind, I'll just put it over here," he answered himself, while laying the gun down gently on the empty bed beside them. "Exactly what went on in here anyway?" he finally asked.

"Actually, I'm still a little weak, and it's a long story..."

"No worries," he assured her, as he clutched her hand again. "You can tell me all about it some other time. You know, before I left, there was something I wanted to tell you. But under the circumstances, I figured it wasn't the right time. When I found out what had happened to you, I was kicking myself for having waited. It taught me that the right time is always *now*."

Eve listened quietly with anticipation, eagerly awaiting his revelation. However, Dan just leaned down and kissed her instead. Right on the lips this time. It was rather brief, but mutually satisfying.

"That's quite the beautiful language, but is there an English translation?" Eve pushed.

The kiss had really been a copout, and they both knew it. Eve obviously wasn't about to let him off the hook either.

"...or is it not *now* yet?" she continued, backing him into a corner.

His instincts were telling him to go into full retreat. Instead, he surrendered unconditionally.

"Yes. I want you to know that I lo..."

"...Dan! Can you clear that bed, so we can lay your prey on it?" Robert interrupted, as he and the other two shuffled in.

Dan looked visibly frustrated as he turned his head back to Eve. She gave him a knowing smile, as if to say, *you tried*. She then pushed his hand away and nodded in the direction of the intruders.

After placing Chad on the bed, Robert used the clinic's P.A. system to summon any available medical staff. He also requested the attendance of the engineers. He wanted them to construct a makeshift prison.

"I know the perfect place for a cell. There's a grotto at the eastern end of the caves, by the river. They just need to insert some bars, run an electric line into it, and voilà – instant dungeon. Tell them I'll be back shortly," he instructed Dan. "I'm going outside to contact Bill and tell them the good news. It's too dangerous to hike down here in the dark though. They can just camp out for the night."

"Will that be safe though?" Dan worried.

"A lot safer than falling from a cliff and breaking your neck. Besides, if I know Bill, he'll stay up all night to watch over your mother."

Dan gave him an approving nod.

Once outside, Robert had no trouble establishing contact with Bill over the walkie-talkie. He could tell from the tone of Bill's voice that he was overjoyed to hear the news.

"*That's a big ten-four! You all have yourselves a good night! Over and out!*"

"Sweet dreams! Over and out!" Robert replied happily.

Chapter Sixteen

Go Fish

Due to the recent events, morale had been exceedingly low amongst the citizenry of Eos. The next morning however, brought with it a renewed sense of hope;
Chad and Ian were now safely contained in the new makeshift dungeon. The engineers had worked through the night to insert bars in the grotto; Eve was making a speedy recovery in the clinic; and at breakfast, Michael had happily shared the details of the restoration at each serving. It had been a labor of love for him to retell the same story over and over.
While he was repeating it for the third time, the guardians were over in the security room, accompanied by Dan's mother and Ryan. Robert was poring over the books Chad had piled up by the monitors. He was especially enthralled by Chief Q's notebook.
"You guys think there really is some loot stashed somewhere in this place?" Robert asked as he turned a page.
His question hadn't been aimed at anyone in particular.
"If there is, it must be really well hidden. We had everyone desperately searching, and nothing's turned up," Ryan reminded him.
"What was Chad's theory?"
"Oh, he thought maybe the Chief had left a note in some aboriginal language, but it just seems like gibberish. Something about animals and such."
"Maybe it's some sort of code," Dan casually offered. "Just like we needed codes to get the fuel, and for gaining entry into Eos," he added, as his mother suddenly walked over to Robert.
"Could I see that notebook?" she asked curiously.
"Sure. Here you go," Robert said as he handed it to her.
"I think my son is right."
Everyone's ears perked up and they turned toward her.
"How so?" Robert asked.
"My husband told me about some code that was used by the military during the second world war."
"My father was that old?" Dan spurted out, rather rudely.
"Oh no," his mother chuckled, "but he *was* a Navajo as you know. He told me about something called the 'code talkers code,' if I remember correctly. They used the Navajo language because no one outside the U.S. would recognize it."
As everyone listened intently, she ran her index finger over the words on the page.
"Yes, that's definitely what this is! And the first step is already done. The words have been translated into English. Now all you do is take the first

letter of each word to form the coded words. Fox is 'F', ice is 'I'...fish farm! It says fish farm! Does that make sense to anyone?"

With excitement in their voices, they all responded affirmatively in their own way. Helen of course, was still unfamiliar with the facility, and the words had meant nothing to her.

"Well done!" Robert rejoiced. "You two make a great team. I guess intelligence can be hereditary."

Dan and his mother simply smiled at each other.

"Okay, let's go treasure hunting," Robert announced. "I'll need someone to stay behind and guard the fort though."

"I'll do it," Bill volunteered. "You youngsters go and have fun."

"Mind if I keep you company? I've already had enough excitement this month," Helen jested.

"It would be my pleasure," Bill said with a warm smile.

The truth is, that the two of them had hit it off quite well. Besides both being widows, they shared many common interests as well. The previous evening in the cave, they had completely lost track of time, as they conversed into the wee hours of the night.

***

By mid-afternoon, the two guardians, along with Michael and Ryan, had completely scoured the environs of the fish farm. None of them had discovered anything unusual, or any signs of buried treasure.

They then turned their attention toward the giant pond itself. It was twenty-five feet in diameter and ten feet deep. It had been carved right out of the rock underneath, then lined with concrete. Roughly two thirds of the water lay beneath ground level. The remainder was contained by the thick concrete walls surrounding the watery pen. The top of the walls came up about shoulder level to an average sized man. Four metal ladders had been embedded around the outside, providing access for the caretaker.

Robert led the other three up a ladder to the surface of the wall. They then stood on the rim, which was about two feet thick. They spread out and walked around the perimeter, gazing into the clear waters below. They couldn't clearly make out the bottom, but there seemed to be nothing more than a drain down there. The sides however, were a different story. The entire pond appeared to be lined, with some type of hatch-like formations. Through the water, they appeared to be made of the same substance as the rest of the pond, cement. Therefore, they were probably no more than decorative in nature. But this was their last remaining lead, and they needed confirmation for, or against their theory.

Dan had been tasked with contacting the caretaker, Farmer Willie, and bringing him back to the pond. When asked the purpose of the square slabs, he informed them that he too was unaware. He *also* assumed that they were ornamental. The entire structure was complete when he took over their maintenance, minus the fish.

He was then asked to drain it, to a level just below the mysterious outcroppings. The process took much longer than the four had hoped, but eventually, they were all laid bare. As they had already noticed long before, the reliefs were indeed made of cement. Robert wasted no time and jumped right in, scaring many of the pond's inhabitants in the process. The trout that were in that side of the enclosure, darted over to the other side. Robert clasped one of the square slabs from the top and bottom and formed a strong grip. To his surprise, and delight, there was obvious movement. They *were* indeed some type of covering.

"It's moving!" he cried out to his companions.

The five grown men all suddenly felt like children on Christmas morning, all brimming with unbridled curiosity. The slabs were basically just giant concrete lids with rubber seals.

"Do you need a hand with that?" Dan offered.

"No," Robert replied with a strained voice, "No sense both of us getting soaked."

As soon as he had spoken, the lid popped off completely, and Robert almost let it fall. He had momentarily underestimated the weight of concrete, even relatively thin slabs of it. After lowering it to the floor, he leaned it against the wall. He immediately realized their suspicions were correct, they had hit the jackpot. As the others looked on with anticipation, Robert inserted both hands into the vault and pulled out a couple of gold bricks. They were covered in clear plastic cases, and there were many more where those came from.

"Is that what it looks like from here?" Michael asked.

"Technically, I'm not a metallurgist, but I'll have to assume we've hit the motherlode." Robert replied.

Altogether, he ended up pulling out two-hundred, one kilogram bars of the precious metal. He then returned them all to their watery lair, leaving the lid off. There were twenty-nine more vaults to open.

"Alright guys, time to get wet!" Robert exclaimed. "Let's get all these babies open and see what else we have here. Willie, would you mind getting some paper and cataloguing the contents?"

"Not at all. I'll be back in ten minutes," He replied enthusiastically.

It took them until just past dinner time to open the remaining compartments, and count up the treasure. They all held the same contents, gold bars, and the exact same amount of them. It wasn't hard to do the math. Two-hundred bars multiplied by thirty; there were six-thousand of the precious bricks in total. While none of them knew exactly what the current price of gold was, they knew they were looking at a few hundred-million dollars' worth.

Interestingly, one of the compartments contained a couple of extra items. There was a long letter and an audio CD, both well sealed in plastic.

Dan had been the one to find these, but he passed them on to Robert and went back to work.

While the others had continued the happy task of totaling up the loot, Robert had read the entire letter. When he was done, Michael had queried him on its contents. All Robert said was that it was written by Katzman, and that he would read it to them later back at the security room. He then excused himself to go and listen to the CD.

Chapter Seventeen

The Veil is Lifted

Those attending the final dinner service, got a bit of a show as well. Michael excitedly recounted the day's events to all at his table. It wasn't long before other diners started to gather around and listen. The news would spread like wildfire, and soon, nearly everyone in Eos already knew about the great discovery.

For Dan, it was an especially pleasant evening. Eve had been released from the clinic only hours earlier, and was enjoying her first cafeteria meal in a few days. Naturally, the two shared the same table, and did more talking than eating. It was not by accident that they had a table all to themselves. Everyone knew that they were somewhat of a couple, and they had afforded Dan and Eve some privacy. A lot had transpired between the time Dan had left and the present. But they had each other pretty much updated, by the time Michael came over.

"Sorry to interrupt guys. I just wanted to see if Dan was interested in heading back to security. Since Robert hasn't shown up yet, I got the chef to make a doggie bag for him. If you want to find out what that letter was all about, you can join me and Ryan. Otherwise, I can just fill you in later."

Personally, Dan would have preferred to stay behind with Eve, but he didn't want to make it too obvious.

"What do you think, Eve? Am I keeping you from anything important? Or maybe I've overtired you. If so, I can go with them and get out of your hair."

"No. Not at all. I feel fine actually. How about if we all go together instead?" she proposed to the three of them.

"If you're feeling up to it, then you're more than welcome," Michael volunteered.

"Great. Let's go then," Dan said cheerfully.

The walk from the cafeteria to the security room is not a long one, since they're both located in the main cavern. Even so, Ryan found it extremely awkward, as everyone was very quiet. Michael had talked himself out over dinner. As for Dan and Eve, they were walking hand in hand, and just basking in each other's glow. Ryan still felt tremendous guilt over his role in the uprising. Although everyone else seemed to have forgiven and forgotten, he hadn't managed to forgive himself. He basically felt unworthy to be in their presence. The only reason he hadn't left Eos yet, was because it might appear like he was running away from his crimes. He figured he should try to earn everyone's trust first. Afterwards, he could probably leave without causing them any worries about confidentiality.

And so, the four of them made their way to the security room, each in their own private world of thought. For the sake of not startling Robert, Michael knocked on the door first before opening it.

"Delivery!" he shouted as he entered, holding up a large, brown paper bag. "It's not like you to miss a meal. Is everything alright?"

"Thanks," Robert said as he accepted Michael's offering. "I was just thinking about this letter and I lost all track of time."

"So, what was that letter all about anyway?" Michael asked.

"Yeah, and what was on the CD?" Dan added.

"The CD is just a copy of the letter actually, narrated by Katzman himself. I've decided I should let everyone hear it," Robert said very somberly.

"Why do I get the feeling it's not a love letter?" Michael teased warily.

"It's pretty mind blowing actually. Listen for yourselves," Robert said as he picked up the mic and pressed the button.

"*Your attention please! I Have an important message for all residents. Please listen carefully to the following recorded address!*"

He then placed the mic close to the computer's speaker, and tapped at the keyboard.

"*Greetings, this is Ronald Katzman. First of all, I'd like to convey my warmest regards to every member of this community. Although many of you probably don't know much about me, I assure you that I know about all of you. I know that each of you is an important piece of the mosaic which is the Eos family.*

Unfortunately for me, if you are reading or listening to this message, then I've probably passed on or become incapacitated. You see, I was supposed to deliver this speech personally. Your wonderful head caretaker, Chief Qaletaqa hasn't yet been given the information I'm about to share with you, and this is just a back-up for him, in case anything should happen to me. Speaking of which, any report of me having had a heart attack or committing suicide are almost certainly not true. But that's not important right now. It's just a minor detail, and I could go on for days relating the entire story. I'm going to give you only the major facts, and the rest is in your hands."

To say that everyone listening had Katzman's full attention, would be an understatement. The residents were all riveted to the spot, regardless of their location.

"*First, I should tell you a little about myself. I can understand how you may think I'm a great philanthropist. But in reality, nothing could be further from the truth. I've spent most of my life taking advantage of people. Most of you probably don't realize it, but this nation is run by a small but very powerful group of people. Until quite recently, I was one of these elites. The reason for this concentration of power is due to our immense wealth. And it's not just a saying that the rich get richer. It's a fact.*

You may have noticed that on paper currency, there's always a letter on the front left side, above the seal. On older notes, these letters are large and are inside the circular seal. In any case, the letters always run from A through L. A few of you may know that these letters signify the various cities where the notes are printed. The letter K for example, represents Dallas. What I'm sure none of you would know, is that these letters also represent names. The names of twelve families. These twelve families basically own all the paper currency in the U.S. Any notes with the letter K on them belong to the Katzman family, of which I am the patriarch."

As he was explaining all this, Eve pulled the five-dollar bill out of her purse. Coincidentally, it had the letter K on it. She held up the money for the others to see, as they continued listening.

"A few years ago, I had a 'road to Damascus' experience, quite literally. I was on my way to the Mid-East to sow some seeds of discontent. As you know, war is a very profitable business. On my flight, I was seated next to Father James, whom you've probably met by now. After introducing ourselves, we began to make small-talk. I told him what I thought he wanted to hear, but he told me things that I needed to hear. And though I've met thousands of people in my lifetime, he was the first person to ever do that.

And so, because of my personal epiphany, I returned home without having carried out my task. My cohorts were none too pleased. Especially when I informed them of my decision to leave the finance world completely. In the eyes of the other eleven, I became a traitor. Unfortunately, I became an outcast even to my own family. The only difference is that my family was willing to live and let live. That wasn't the case with my banking associates. They made it quite clear to me, that the only way out is through death, natural or otherwise. By walking away from my past life, I have also made a huge economic sacrifice. It has cost me billions of dollars. But in the end, I feel it was all worth the price I've had to pay.

Eventually, I ended up coming to this area for a personal hiatus, and managed to bump into Chief Q. We ended up getting to know each other very well, and sharing our innermost secrets. Needless to say, the Chief was quite shocked with what I told him. However, his plan to create Eos came as quite a revelation to me as well. We had obviously come from two very different paths, but fate had brought us together somehow.

I'm very grateful that I managed to squirrel away enough to sustain Eos for years to come. Although, the real asset of Eos could prove to be the seedbank. After all, you can't eat gold.

Which brings me to my second main disclosure; the real reason why you've all been brought here. Now, it's possible that some natural disaster may have indeed occurred. In which case, this would serve as a good practice run. However, you need to know what those in power have planned, and all the pieces are now in place. They call it Operation Sundown. The next time a large solar flare threatens the earth, they will use it as a trigger to commence with their scheme. If one doesn't occur within a certain time frame, they will resort to Plan B. That would involve staging an EMP attack, and blaming terrorists."

Of course, the tycoon couldn't have foreseen both happening, as had been the case.

"The aim of this shadow government is to herd the entire population into the major coastal cities, where they can be more easily controlled. With the exception of those in rural areas, who are tied to the land and are self-reliant, most people will eventually migrate out of necessity. They will be lured by the promise of food and electricity, especially once winter sets in. Many will believe it is a temporary solution, but I assure you, the authorities have no intention of restoring full power. Those citizens tending the agricultural areas will essentially be turned into serfs. Any farmers not cooperating with the government will be seen as traitors, and will be removed and replaced. The crops which are produced will not be distributed fairly, or as needed. In the cities, hunger, disease and violence will become widespread.

In short, the ultimate goal of this powerful cabal is to reduce our nation's population by about ninety percent. They will then come out of their underground lairs, and dwell in their newly created utopia. I know it must be hard for many of you to fully grasp this reality..."

One such person was undoubtedly Jack, the Vietnam vet who was inside his abode listening with his wife. The thought of his own government betraying him was infuriating.

"I can't believe what I'm hearing!" he fumed. I served this country faithfully for over forty-five years! How did we get to this point?"

"Settle down dear. You're going to give yourself a heart attack," Marie said in a caring but firm tone.

As if in answer to Jack's concern, Katzman addressed the topic;

"...Now, don't think for a minute that everyone in government is corrupt and evil. Most of them don't really know what they're involved with. It's very compartmentalized and on a need-to-know basis. These individuals believe they're serving their country honestly. It is they who will become our greatest weapon in this fight. However, educating them will not be an easy task. Most of them will view us as traitors or rebels.

In conclusion, that brings us to the reason you are all here. Eos was not created to serve as a survival camp. That would be a very selfish and eventually futile exercise. It is meant to be more like a training center. As you know, you have all been selected in accordance with your skills, knowledge and abilities, as well as the required ethical traits.

Some of you are elderly; but your experience and acquired knowledge are essential building blocks of this community. Some of you are just starting to raise families; your main task will be to rear upstanding young citizens, capable of perpetuating the ideals of our noble endeavor. Some of you are young and single; it is your duty to go out into the world and spread the news to as many as possible. You will be our front-line soldiers in this battle. I would like to conclude, by thanking each and every one of you for your service. May you all be blessed with peace and freedom. Thank you."

You could have heard a pin drop in the security room, as Katzman had left everyone in a collective stupor.

"Wow," exclaimed Michael in a subdued tone.

"Wow indeed," seconded Robert, in between bites of his chicken Caesar.

"I guess I've just been given my marching orders," Dan stated.

"I didn't hear anything about gender, so consider me drafted," added Eve.

Her announcement didn't surprise Dan in the least, nor anyone else for that matter. Ryan was more than okay with the idea of leaving. It would do away with the awkwardness he felt here, as well as provide an opportunity for redemption. As for Helen, although she was thankful for having been brought to Eos, she couldn't help but feel anxious and fearful for the future. She wasn't so worried about herself as much as for the others, especially Dan.

"I just can't understand why some people have a need to control everyone else. This world would be so much better if we just shared its abundance and looked out for each other," she lamented.

"Indeed," Robert agreed again, between another bite of his salad.

Chapter eighteen

Requiem

The early Autumn sunlight gleamed off the white sandstone cliffs in the background. High above the expansive backyard of the Katzman residence, a bald eagle circled lazily overhead. The apt symbolism would not have been lost on Chief Q. In fact, it probably wasn't; it was he whom everyone had gathered to bid a final farewell to. The Italian style garden made for a lovely little cemetery, and not by chance. It had been intended for such a use. Only, no one expected it to be needed this soon.

Beside two freshly dug graves lay two simple Spruce caskets. Both were adorned with wreaths of Fern, Honeysuckle, Jewel flowers and other native species. The only difference was that one had a portrait of Chief Q. below the wreath, wearing a full ceremonial head-dress. It made him look so much more dignified than he normally did. But, in his humility, he had always preferred to blend in with everyone else. To his right, lay the mortal remains of the hermit, Johnny. They had carefully excavated him from the mound of dirt and gravel where he'd been found.

Most of the attendees didn't appear to be dressed for a funeral. But to be fair, the idea had probably never crossed their minds at the time they were packing. Two exceptions were Rabbi Yosef and Father James, who were both garbed in their traditional black outfits. After various prayers and blessings had been offered, it was left to Father James to do the Eulogy. Due to the risk of being spotted by outsiders, the entire ceremony was more rushed than was merited by the occasion.

Without having any type of sound-system at his disposal, Father James would have to rely on his ability to project his voice. And so, he invited everyone to move up as close as possible. Robert, Michael, and some of the various caretakers were right at the front of the crowd. Dan and Eve stood together directly behind them, while Ryan meandered around the rear of the group. He had been tasked with security detail; or rather, he had volunteered. Ryan had vowed to himself that he would somehow make up for his past sins.

"There is no greater love than this, that a man should lay down his life for his friends," commenced Father James. "There are a lot of people who can quote scripture word for word. Unfortunately, the number who can live it is probably far fewer. I doubt Chief Qaletaqa could quote many scriptures, but I know for a fact, that he lived them. He was a simple man, and the *commandments* are simple; to love God, and your neighbor as yourself. Of course, carrying that out is not always easy. But, we know from Chief Q's example, that it's possible. I could go on all day about what a wonderful human being he was. Heck, I could spend hours just recounting his corny jokes. But for those of you who didn't know him very well, I can encapsulate his life in a riddle that I made in his honor; why did Chief Q cross our path? To get us to the other side."

Everyone in the crowd smiled, and some even giggled.

"Today, we are also laying to rest the hermit, Johnny. A man I know very little about. All I know of him, I learned from the young guardian, Daniel. By his accounts, Johnny was probably suffering from a mental illness of some sort, but Dan was able to see past that and find his humanity. I can't help but recall the passage where Jesus says, '...I was a stranger and you welcomed me.' From what I hear, they don't come much stranger than Johnny."

Again, the priest had managed to bring a collective smile to the faces of the attendees. As for Dan, he couldn't help wondering how Johnny could have known about Chad. Whether it was pure coincidence, or intuition, no one would ever know for sure. He also remembered how Johnny had let him keep the spearhead, as a remembrance. He intended to treasure it forever, along with Chief Q's prayer feather.

"As you know, we are pressed for time due to security reasons, so I'll have to keep this short. Consider it a blessing. This is the part of the eulogy where I usually break into my tone-deaf version of, 'Somewhere over the rainbow,'" Father James joked to audible laughter. "For those of you who may be offended by my seeming lack of respect, I apologize, but I'm Irish, and that's how we roll. To us, funerals and births are very similar occasions. They both signify the beginning of a new life, and should be celebrated. In closing, I'd like to call down God's blessings on everyone here, as I now leave you to grieve privately in your own ways. Thank you."

As the mourners began to trickle back into their underground lair, the caretakers quickly began to lower the coffins into their respective resting places. With the help of their mini bulldozer, they had the graves filled in and covered up in no time.

Eve had an appointment with the doctor, who wanted to follow up on her condition, and so she excused herself promptly. Father James had remained, along with his pal, Rabbi Yosef. Dan had also stayed behind. He had wanted to speak privately with the priest, but he didn't want to disturb their quiet time at the graves, and so he waited until the two began to walk away. He intercepted them, halfway between the fresh plots and the entrance to the underground.

"Hi Dan," Rabbi Yosef greeted.

"Good morning sirs," Dan replied. "I wanted to speak with you Father. Would now be a good time?"

"Certainly," said the priest.

"I'll leave you two alone," offered the rabbi.

"Oh, you don't have to do that," Dan insisted. "I wouldn't mind getting *your* advice as well."

"So, what's on your mind young man?" probed Father James.

"A couple of things. First, I assume you both heard Mr. Katzman's request for single people to go back to the cities?"

"Yes," Father James acknowledged, as Rabbi Yosef nodded affirmatively.

"Well, Eve and I are leaving along with any other volunteers..."

"That must have been tough news for your mother to hear, I'm assuming," interjected Father James.

"Yeah, she was sad to hear she'd be losing me again so soon. Ryan tried his best to console her though. He promised to protect us with his life, and bring us back safe and sound. The second thing is what I was needing some advice with," Dan added with visible apprehension.

"We'd be glad to help, if we can," said the rabbi.

"I'm not sure if either of you are aware, but Eve and I have developed a relationship over the past few weeks..." Dan said to test the waters.

"I think I speak for almost everyone when I say; it's becoming rather obvious," Father James said bluntly, but with an understanding grin.

"I was thinking of asking her to marry me," Dan spurted out.

"That's great!" exclaimed Father James, as the two men smiled and patted Dan on the shoulders.

"So, you don't think it's bad timing? I mean, with all that's going on right now?"

"Certainly not," said Rabbi Yosef. "I mean if you were inquiring about having an actual wedding, I would have to advise against it. But as long as you don't have a set timetable, I don't see any problem."

"I totally agree," concurred the priest.

"I hope Eve likes the idea as much as you two," Dan replied with a suddenly more upbeat demeanor. "I'm not even able to give her a proper engagement ring right now. All I can offer her is my football championship ring from high school. It's probably worth fifty bucks; pretty ironic considering she's a jeweller."

"The way I see it, if she turns you down because of the ring, then she's probably more in love with the idea of a wedding than with you," Rabbi Yosef stated frankly.

"The problem is, she claims to be a shallow person. Although I strongly disagree with her assessment," Dan opined.

"Either way, it'll be a good test for the both of you," concluded the rabbi.

"Actually, I have a solution for that," said Father James. "If you're free for a moment, could you come up to my quarters? Or, down to my quarters, as the case may be."

"Sure, I was just going for lunch anyway. I could always go for the one o'clock serving instead," Dan replied with a look of curiosity.

The trio entered the caverns together, and made their way down the stairs. At the ground level, they parted ways; the rabbi to the cafeteria, and the other two up the path to the suites.

When Rabbi Yosef entered the dining room, he was greeted by Robert and Ryan. The two had set up a small table just outside the doorway, to his right. Together, the two were essentially a mobile draft office. Ryan recorded names and short bios, as Robert briefed the recruits on the upcoming mission. They hadn't set a departure date yet, or target cities, but were hoping to leave as soon as possible. Transportation certainly wouldn't be a problem. Every time Robert asked for volunteers to lend their vehicles, everyone in the room with a vehicle had raised their hands. *Jack* had even insisted on being enlisted, but between his wife and Robert, he never stood a chance. Robert greatly admired his spunk however, and made a point of thanking him for his patriotism.

At the clinic, Eve was in the process of receiving a clean bill of health. But the doctor warned her to take it easy, for at least a couple of weeks.

Over in Father James abode, Dan perused the décor as the priest fumbled through a drawer. On top of the modest dresser sat a wooden crucifix. On the wall to his left, Dan noticed a picture of Mother Teresa. He actually knew who *she* was, as opposed to the man on the opposite wall. That fellow had a longish, salt and pepper beard, and looked like some sort of hillbilly priest or monk.

"Ah, here it is," Father James said gleefully.

As he turned around, all Dan could see was some small, white cloth, bunched up in his hands. After giving the contents a few rubs, Father James opened the cloth to reveal a diamond ring.

"I've never had it appraised, and I don't even know how many karats it is, but it seems substantial enough for even the shallowest young maiden," Father James said playfully.

"Whoa, it certainly does! That would be perfect. But I can't afford something like that, and what little money I do have, is frozen in the bank."

"Dan, you and Eve have more than earned it already. Besides, it was never meant to be sold anyway."

He then went on to recount how it had come into his possession. Many years back, a cancer-ridden widow had given it to him on her deathbed. Apparently, she had no one to hand it down to. She asked Father James to take it, and pass it along to whomever he felt was deserving of it.

"Over the years, I've had several opportunities to give it away. But it never quite felt like the right time, until now."

And with that, he extended his hands forward, and Dan accepted his offering, in awe.

"I don't know what to say... thank you so much."

Dan held up the ring and slowly rotated his hand. Even in the soft lighting, it still managed to throw off a series of sparkling winks.

Epilogue

Four days had now passed since the funeral service. Under the cover of morning darkness, a steady stream of cars trickled out from the underground parking. Leading the procession was Ryan, in the black Hummer. His was the only vehicle with the headlights on. Two days earlier, a destination had been decided upon; Corpus Christi, Texas.

The city had been chosen for many reasons. For one, it was not too distant, an approximate eleven to twelve-hour drive from Eos. Also, winter was not too far off, and they needed to take climate into consideration. Being in an inland area in winter with no electricity, could only add to their hardship. They would have to literally work their way up from the bottom, geographically speaking. Hopefully, they could educate and enlist large numbers of followers in the Lone Star State. After all, Texans were known for being freedom loving mavericks.

Lastly, it was chosen for tactical reasons. Three people in their contingent were from the area. One was a ham radio enthusiast, with many fellow 'Hammers' throughout the south. To avoid any possible detection of Eos, the plan was to stop a few hours out, then try to make contact with other operators. The van he was riding in, carried all the necessary equipment. The fellow claimed he could set up a portable station in minutes. Robert was very aware of the value of ham radio. As a marine, he had been deployed to Louisiana to help with the Katrina relief effort. There, he'd learned that in many areas, amateur radio was the only form of communication left. The lifeline to first responders had proven vital.

At the back of the line, Robert sat at the wheel of Eve's BMW, with the engine running. Dan and Eve were the very last to depart. They had finally finished exchanging farewells with Bill and Helen, a tearful affair for Dan's mother.

"You two find your way back here real soon!" Bill called out, "so we can throw you a nice wedding, you hear?"

Maybe a double wedding, Dan thought to himself as he waved. Bill and his mother had bonded amazingly well in the short time since they'd met. Dan was very happy about it, and it made it a little easier to leave Helen so abruptly. Bill would be the temporary head of the guardians, until Robert returned. He, along with all the caretakers, would share in the leadership of Eos, now that Chief Q was gone.

Eve was smiling from ear to ear, as Dan joined her in the backseat. She looked unusually fresh for someone who couldn't get to sleep the night before. Dan had dropped in after his evening rounds, which wasn't unusual, but his purpose had been very special this time.

While proposing to her, he made it clear that she should feel no obligation whatsoever. If she wanted to get to know him better, or she felt it was bad timing due to the circumstances, then he was perfectly fine with that. No hard feelings. She had thought about it for no more than two or three seconds, before accepting the ring. The speed of her decision had surprised not only Dan, but even Eve herself.

"You'll never believe what I discovered last night," she said excitedly as she closed the door.

"What is it?" Dan wondered curiously, as she twisted off her engagement ring.

"Well, being a jeweller, I couldn't help but wonder about this ring's origins. So, I took out my loupe, and searched for a hallmark of some kind..."

"A hallmark?"

"Yeah, that's a small engraving on fine jewellery that provides info about where and when an item was made, who made it, or what it's made of. Most pieces have three or four different hallmarks. Anyway, I found a very familiar sponsor's mark in it. It's the letter 'D' in a distinct Celtic font. That just happens to be the hallmark of Donegan Jewellers!" Eve shared, as she held

up the ring in front of Dan's bewildered eyes. He couldn't make out anything, especially in the early morning light, but he would take her word for it.

"Unbelievable," Robert said, after overhearing the conversation from the front seat.

For his part, Dan was speechless.

"My father designed this ring back in 1974, one of his earliest creations. I have no way to verify it, but it's possible that this is the very first ring he ever made," Eve emphasized, by shaking her hand as she clasped the ring.

"After all that's happened in the last few weeks," Dan declared, "I wouldn't doubt it for a second."

A reverent silence descended on the car, as the three occupants all contemplated recent happenings, each in their own way. After putting the ring back in its rightful place, Eve exchanged a sincere smile with Dan and the two shared a quick kiss. She then rested her head on his right shoulder. Within moments, she was sound asleep.

Dan stared out into the eastern sky, where the sun was just about to make its majestic entrance. It was heralded, by a royal court of gold and silver-lined clouds, awaiting the crown jewel. How many other magical moments lay in store for them? To be designed, crafted, and inlaid into their paths? Only the Master Goldsmith knows.

Made in the USA
Columbia, SC
27 April 2017